Double Take

June Oldham

Double Take

VIKING KESTREL

VIKING KESTREL

Published by the Penguin Group
27 Wrights Lane, London W8 5TZ, England
Viking Penguin Inc., 40 West 23rd Street, New York, New York 10010, USA
Penguin Books Australia Ltd, Ringwood, Victoria, Australia
Penguin Books Canada Ltd, 2801 John Street, Markham, Ontario, Canada L3R 1B4
Penguin Books (NZ) Ltd, 182–190 Wairau Road, Auckland 10, New Zealand

Penguin Books Ltd, Registered Offices: Harmondsworth, Middlesex, England

First published 1988

Copyright © June Oldham, 1988

Filmset in Linotron 202 Melior

Typeset, printed and bound in Great Britain by
Hazell Watson & Viney Limited
Member of BPCC plc
Aylesbury Bucks

British Library Cataloguing in Publication Data
Oldham, June
Double take.
I. Title
823'.914 [F]

ISBN 0-670-82088-1

For Judith Beattie

Chapter One

With legs soaking in four inches of tepid water and trunk upright, Olivia attempted to savour one of her lodgings' more neglected antiquities. Fashioned like a hip-bath, its deep belly supported on wide, clawed feet, it stood majestic in the middle of the room and beguiled with the promise of an opulent wallow. But this was spurious. As soon as she had climbed in, hopeful for total immersion, the brass tap shaped like a well-nourished mermaid bearing an H tattooed on her tail, had been taken by a paroxysm of belching, emitted a final squirt and dried up. Fortunately this disappointment had a compensation for when Olivia had paddled through the shallows and closed the valve, the pipes along the route from the basement had halted their rattle, the shudders under the floorboards had been reduced to mere quivers and the house was at last still.

Quickly, before the surface could harden to ice, Olivia smeared soap on that half of her body grounded above tide level and rinsed it off in a pool between her feet. This done, she rested her nape upon the lip of the bath and contemplated the fluff which whiskered the plaster-rose in the ceiling, looped the electric wire and topped the glass shade with a felt cap. Now that the bathroom had been opened up for her use – her landlady declaring a preference for a strip wash at the sink – Olivia wondered whether cleaning it were her responsibility, though she did not imagine that was an issue to have engaged Mrs Winterton's thoughts; she had an almost devout tolerance of dust probably because, as she would

1

remark, it was the simple matter to which we shall all be reduced. Nevertheless Olivia thought she might have a go at removing it. That would be one way of passing the time. To have a bath was another, but there was a limit to how long she could bear to sit marinating her legs in a trough of lukewarm, slightly moist silt. And there was a lot of time to pass.

The possibility of a reprieve was signalled by the telephone's clang in the hall and, over the last six months programmed more acutely to its sound than she had ever been to an alarm clock, Olivia was out of the bath before the second ring. Bibbing her front with a towel and forcing wet feet into pumps gave her just enough time to acknowledge the convenience of a bathrobe behind an uncurtained window, and the sprint down the passage and stairs provided another two seconds for listing the callers: Yorkshire Television ('Emmerdale Farm', five lines); Video Training Film (waitress); RSC (Dorcas, shepherdess in *The Winter's Tale*, and unspecified understudying); Octagon Theatre (dance-tap in new musical); The Monstrous Regiment (community tour). The half-dozen steps along the hall to the telephone allowed her to work out, in the event of a choice, her preference: the last, she decided, as picking up the handset she gave her number.

'I'm pleased that I've found you in,' her mother greeted.

'I'm not,' then hastily clarified with: 'I'd rather not be hanging about.'

'Still resting, then?' The inverted commas round the second word were as arch as a trendy expression from the pulpit. Though not wholly reconciled to the occupation of her daughter, Mrs Quinn could not resist some of the reflected glamour she believed it conferred and she had been quick to adopt its vocabulary. *Resting* gratified her; it was so much more admissible than *unemployed*.

Irritated, Olivia said, 'Yes; I'm still out of work.'

'Didn't the part in television come off, then? I was phoning to inquire the time. I thought you said tonight.' The tone was alarmed and slightly resentful. As soon as this conversation was over she must dash round to neighbours, telephone friends, contact the milkman, paper boy, Olivia's former headmaster, cancelling all the excitement she had spent a week drumming up. Her daughter was tempted to let this happen but the desire for fame, however parochial, won.

'Yes; it's going out tonight after the local news, but it doesn't count.'

'Your first television appearance, and you say it doesn't count!' Her mother pretended bewilderment, and there were crackles and thuds. Olivia could see her at the other end, lifting the telephone off the table and sinking to the floor, weak with relief. 'I'm surprised you can be so modest, Olivia.'

Not so long ago you had advised that. 'There's nothing to boast about. It's not a *part*. I don't have anything to say.'

'That doesn't matter, dear. Being there on the screen is what's important. Who knows, somebody might see you and say, "That's just the young woman I want for such and such." '

It was necessary to suppress the hope. 'I've told you what it is, Mother: not a part, a representation.'

'And that's enough. Thousands of people will be watching. I can vouch for several dozen myself.' Olivia had been right. 'We shall all be switching on at seven, waiting impatiently for them to get through the boring bits until it's "Mystery of the Week".'

'It's a very short mystery; it takes all of two minutes.'

'A person's future can be decided in less,' Mrs Quinn philosophized. Then predictably, 'It's a shame you couldn't visit. We could have all watched it together and gone for a little celebration afterwards.' Showing her off.

'You can do that anyway. I must go back to the bathroom, Mother.' She knew better than to mention that she was standing there with only a towel between her and two clear panes of glass in the front door, incongruous replacements within the bowing and cracked mosaic of leaded lights. 'I have to smarten up for Judy. She's coming this evening.'

'I see.' A mistress of the pregnant monosyllable, Olivia's mother conveyed what she saw: that, despite her offer to pay the fare, her invitation had been declined in favour of an evening with a friend. 'Well, as we settle down we'll think of the two of you watching.'

'I shouldn't bother. I'll be meeting Judy at the time.'

'Fancy making you miss the film! We'll record it for you, then you can see it next time you're home.'

'Thanks, but I've just started to rent a video-recorder. According to Equity I can set it against income tax.'

Mrs Quinn laughed. 'That's a good idea. And you'll be subject to tax soon, with many more film parts like this!'

Eighty pounds.

'Is that all? Mervyn picked up two hundred and twenty-five.' Outside the coach station Judy paused beside a bin lapped by the rubbish of other travellers and deposited the gnawed peel of a grapefruit and a crumpled tin of Coke. Unimpeded, they hit the bottom.

Olivia said, 'This was only a morning and it wasn't Central. Mervyn's was a speaking part, too.'

'Don't remind me. One line. You'd have thought it was Hamlet, the fuss he made of it. Look, I argued, given that you have to do it straight, there are no more than ten or twelve ways you could possibly deliver it. ''The boss wants to know, Mrs Hinckley, whether you've settled on Passion Pink gloss with a hint of purple on the ceiling or Mirage Mist with a touch of sand on the walls.'' For example, I told him, you could do it like Brando: "The bors he, ugh, ugh, wanna sorta, ugh ugh, know, ugh, Mrs . . ." '

'Or Gielgud, mellifluously: "The boss wisshshsehes to knoooooooow . . ." '

'Exactly. A pity the actual line was: "I've brought some colour cards for you to choose the paint, Mrs Hinckley,'' but he enjoyed the anguish.'

'Oh, Judy!' After the past weeks the other's company was refreshing. 'Anyway, I would have enjoyed some anguish. All I had to do was dash out of a house, down the path, slam the gate and disappear up the street.'

'You could have tried one of John Cleese's funny walks.'

'No chance. There was nothing to go on; no character, no situation. Nothing. I was there merely as a look-alike of another woman.'

'Spooky.'

'Not at all. The whole thing was a non-event. They didn't even provide the clothes. I had to wear my own. It's their attempt to jazz up the local news. Pathetic. Some hick producer with no budget but ambitions to film the next John le Carré decides to practise with a sort of down-market "Crime Watch". Did you see any of that series? Well, think of it without the banks of telephones or the operations-room policemen selected by Scotland Yard's casting director for their appearance of integrity and compassion, and imagine it without the research, presenters or important story, and you've got "Mystery of the Week".'

'I can't wait to see it, particularly since your account doesn't square with Alan's. He was in raptures getting the job. Rang me straight away. He must have blown the fee on the call.'

'He had more latitude.'

'Which no doubt he took.' They giggled. 'Why?'

'Because he wasn't representing a named person. When the agency sent in my photograph – Claire was in the office that day – she suggested Alan for the Telecom fellow who's supposed to be the last one to have seen me – the woman. She's called Elizabeth Drew. The casting assistant was only too happy to have another locally based actor since that cut down travelling expenses. Alan could play it more or less as he liked, whereas I had to keep the character neutral otherwise I might have prejudiced the viewers' response.'

'Sounds difficult and hardly worth it for such a crummy programme.'

'A matter of professionalism.'

'I hope it was appreciated. The job's not the kind to attract ecstatic notices, is it? You were just a cipher. Like being part of an identity parade.'

'Not a part; all of it. And that's what I've been saying. I was employed merely in the hope that some people would be reminded of somebody else. Worse than being an understudy. I wouldn't have done it if I hadn't been rotting from inactivity.'

'I know.'

'There's been nothing since last October, Judy. I've been put up for several parts and I write round to remind directors of my existence, after which I can't think of anything more I can do. You were – what? – three months, before this Assistant Stage Manager job came up.'

'Correct. I was beginning to wonder whether I had chosen the wrong occupation.'

'What's the alternative?'

'Haven't you heard the rumour that the theatre's not the only way of earning a living? Or, in the majority of cases, of not earning a living. I've thought that some time we ought to test the truth of it.'

'We both have: waitressing, charring. You did that courier job.'

'I'm ignoring those because they're automatic. There are so many out-of-work actors serving bars you'd think bar-tending was an apprenticeship for the stage. If it turns them to drink, it is. No; we should be more imaginative and, as well as that, find some way of cashing in on our talents.'

'You're not suggesting Strippergrams?'

'No, but something along those lines, something where we could go in as actresses, supplying a need. There must be thousands of needs waiting to be tapped.'

'Yeah. Let's think . . . My Aunt Fay used to complain about the necessity to attend parent–teacher evenings. Having five children, she was obliged to turn up at some school or other almost monthly. What about HIRE A MOTHER? We wouldn't have to know anything about the kids concerned but just dress marvellously and flirt with all the male members of staff.'

'You've got it! "RENT-A-MUM . . . and forget those tedious evenings showing a brave face in the school assembly hall. Instead, put your son's future in the hands of England's answer to Jane Fonda." We could offer a real service to women here, Olivia. It's not help with the housework they want because they can find ways of avoiding that; nor is it help with the cooking and ironing because there are always frozen fish fingers and radiators that'll dry a shirt reasonably flat. It's the social chores that are less easy to evade and all the duties to Janet and John's education: cubs and brownies, football and violin, extra French and dancing classes.'

'We could do RENT-A-MUM for school prize-givings, swimming galas, sports days, birthday parties, hospital visits, carol services, school plays.'

'We're on! If ever we're out of work at the same time we'll have a go. Which reminds me. Fran says that Common Weal are looking for jugglers. I thought of you but decided you couldn't meet the requirements: male and black. Quite apart from the fact you can't juggle.'

7

'That does seem to cut me out, but thanks for the thought.'

'Any time. Olivia, I know you aren't exactly flush at the moment but couldn't we take a bus?'

'There aren't any. Which allows you more leisure to savour the town's distinctive features.'

'I've seen them all before, elsewhere. One town's neglected back streets are pretty much the same as another's. These houses haven't deteriorated naturally, you know; they were specially built like this as suitable habitations for students, first-generation immigrants, one-parent families, supplementary benefit claimants and out-of-work actresses. It's a reproduction of where I live. Apart from the distinctive feature of – *don't look round*,' she hissed, 'a kerb crawler.'

Though her experience of stage crises was small, Olivia obeyed this directive with the phlegm of an old trouper left holding up the set. 'I hadn't noticed. Why not look?' she demanded.

'I think it's best to seem unconcerned.'

'It sounds to me that you make a habit of this.'

'Formed in France, as a matter of fact. Summer evenings, instead of exercising the dog. Except in some notable areas, I find it less popular in England, don't you? Have you come across this nasty on wheels before?'

'I haven't come across any in this town. Somehow it doesn't seem its style. However, we're only four doors from home.'

'Don't stop. Go past it.'

'Whatever for?'

'Haven't you any sense? So that he doesn't find out where you live.'

'And we walk the streets till he runs out of petrol?' She realized that they were speaking in whispers. 'You're mad, Judy,' she shouted. 'Wonderfully, wonderfully mad. Come on.' Released by the ring of her voice, she grabbed the other's hand and pulled her swiftly along the cracked pavement, round the slumped and rotting gate, up the five feet of path and the four abrupt steps. 'Now give him the two fingers,' she yelled.

Flushed, their shoes rocking on the eroded stone, backs flattened against the creaking glass of the door, they looked down, but the car had gone. Leaving the throb of its engine in their ears and a dryness in their throats.

Olivia opened her handbag and trawled for her key, conscious that she fumbled. Judy said, 'A pity we didn't get his number.'

'I'm not likely to want to look him up.' She felt ridiculous now; the sprint had been childish.

'It would've been a useful check if it happens again. You could report him.'

'You seem to have developed a taste for the sensational.' Her words were pitched to the squeak of the key as she scratched round the lock. 'This is Brick Street — not a tatty thriller.'

Judy sucked in her cheeks and examined the chipped dado along the passage walls, the marble-topped washstand on which stood the telephone, a constellation of finger-marks on its dulled surface. And Olivia thought, she's anxious and I'm snapping, because of a kerb crawler.

'Forget him,' she said. 'Feel like spaghetti lightly smeared with mince? I'm down here, in the basement.'

But as she followed her, Judy added, 'It's significant, isn't it, that we both say "him"?'

'I'll say it is. It signifies the practice of certain men.'

'But neither of us *saw*. In spite of that, we make the assumption. Which is as sexist as a man's taking it for granted that Nurse Smith is a woman.'

They had reached the bottom of the steps. Above their heads a pane of glass tufted with moss sieved the light.

'Hardly. Have you met any women kerb crawlers?'

'Not as far as I know.' She hesitated as if there were

more she wished to say, but seeing Olivia's hand round the knob of her door she was recalled by her sense of the occasion to: 'I hope you can rustle up a couple of glasses. I've brought a bottle of plonk. Courtesy of our very own artistic director. Or it might have been had he known about it. There's to be a reception for civic dignitaries on Thursday, first night, and I reckon it's stage management's duty to ensure that they don't stumble home to their beds pissed out of their tiny minds. This place would make a marvellous set, Olivia,' looking round the room. 'It's like a crypt. All it needs is a coffin.'

'Don't mention that to Mrs Winterton; she might oblige. I see it more as a dungeon with a few arbitrary mod. cons., i.e. a cooker but no sink; an ironing board but no iron; a kitchen table but no stool. Help yourself to the sofa. It's improved since I extracted its single spring.'

'Thanks. Christ! I can feel you're keeping up with your hobbies. Whenever I'm requested to level up an old settee I ask, "Do you want me to stuff it or gut it?" The latter because of you.'

They laughed and thus the pulse of the car at their backs was silenced.

Much later, at the end of a quite different topic, Judy conceded, 'I don't expect there can be many women stupid enough to invite a man into their car.'

'Judy, stop brooding! Any woman capable of doing that must surely also be capable of looking after herself.'

'I wasn't thinking of quite that situation, though.' She paused, then, 'But yes, I suppose you're right. Which poses the question, am I capable of looking after myself? It was through my giving Alan a lift in the theatre van that the thing with him started.'

Olivia grinned. 'When is he collecting?'

'Half eleven, which is four hours after he wished.

Where do you wash up?' The offer was made not in order to tidy the room but to resist the scurrying time.

To Olivia the crusted soup bowls and plates, the empty bottle, wine glasses and used pans were mementoes of her guest to be hoarded. 'In the kitchen. Tomorrow.'

'In that case, why don't we look at the recording of this "Mystery of the Week"? Round off the evening with some light entertainment.'

'If you insist.'

Switching on the machine she pressed the review button and they peered at the figures tugged backwards across the screen, the limbs jerked in a slapstick race: Alan, his lighted cigarette doused by his companion's match before his feet hauled him to the front of the Telecom van; Olivia, her hair swinging at her nape and heels going like pistons pulled towards them, her hand lifted to a gate which closed loudly before opening for her to back in, her face to them now, intense, and her body sucked up the path and into the front door of a house in which furniture rotated; another face staring; then a wink, more furniture static and polished.

Olivia stopped the tape. 'There you are. You've seen it.'

'Very enjoyable, but I'd like to study the way you bang the gate. Do you mind running it through forward, normal speed?'

'I'll let you have my autograph, too, if you like. I've been practising it for my fans,' but she complied. At last accepting that she must watch herself, Olivia felt her bowels contract as if she were going on stage. Such nerves were incongruous to this fleeting appearance.

'You've seen yourself on video plenty of times,' Judy remonstrated above an advertisement for Unbeatable Bargains in Bedroom Accessories. 'We learned a lot from it, especially in the second year.'

'I shan't learn anything from this except not to do it again.'

'You're not likely to be invited. You can't be many women's double. I'm not taken with this voice-over, are you? I certainly wouldn't choose it as a bedroom accessory however much of a bargain it was.'

Tittering, Olivia felt the muscles relax and was grateful.

The display of bedroom furniture snapped off and the same voice continued, 'Pennine News now brings you "Mystery of the Week".'

'Did they have to use him again?'

'Of course. He's Ron Hawksworth. Never off the job.'

'Well, his talent's thin enough to spread easily. Looks as if they spread the advertisements as well,' Judy observed as, reminiscent of a promotion for brown bread, the title sequence of cobbled streets came up. 'All it needs now is a creaking inn sign. I'm really gripped.'

Ron Hawksworth's voice was intoning, 'This week's mystery centres on the whereabouts of a young girl aged seventeen. Here is a photograph taken several years ago.'

Dropped on a wet cobble, a transparency curled to its shape, expanded, flattened, took on opaque colour and filled the screen as the street disappeared.

'The director's got style,' Judy approved.

'Yes; but no script.'

Information was sonorously listed: her name, the town where she lived, the street where she was last seen, not far from where they sat; while the face regarded them as it had regarded a school photographer four years earlier, suspicious, sullen, defying the camera's eye.

'Had you seen that?'

'No, of course not. I just filmed my bit. They didn't even tell me what she's called.'

The tense privacy of the face accused them; watching, they were associated with its loss.

'He says her name is Rita Dale.'

'Yes,' and Olivia was touched with the useless impulse to lean forward and give the girl hers.

The face receded and its stillness was replaced by a frenzy of whirling objects, the film accelerating to a carousel spin, conveying vertiginous panic, before it slowed down and jumped about the debris of a fractured bedroom, its abrupt cuts suggesting haste; then tracking round more leisurely, the camera closed upon details, nosed out their damage, withdrew but unsatiated returned, no longer recording but engaged in a complicity with the violence of the knife that had sliced into a cushion, with the invasion of the hands upon bras and panties dangling from open drawers.

'Clever but horrible,' Judy gasped. 'You'd have thought her parents would have tidied up before this lot reached it.'

'This isn't their house. It's where she was living with Elizabeth Drew. Here.' The room slid away and a terrace of stone houses took its place.

'It was in this street that the scene you have just witnessed occurred,' Ron Hawksworth stated, underlying the director's intention that they should believe they had seen the actual incident. 'It is thought to be connected with Rita's disappearance. Though there is no evidence, to date, of any attack, there is someone who might be able to help clear up our mystery of the week.'

'It belongs to them, does it? How desperate can you get?'

'Exactly,' Olivia agreed. 'It's their attempt to introduce a little drama into the local news, and I don't suppose they'd get police clearance if what they've shown had any importance.'

The camera had selected one of the houses and was

skidding up a short path towards the front door. It climbed the steps, reached the knocker, then swung down, resting on the ground below like a glance from someone standing on the top step. Because of the slope of the land, the ground floor at the front of the house was four feet above the path and, level with the middle step, the cellar window reflected the weeds not a foot from its glass before descending into a narrow twilit well slimed with leaves.

'Like your place,' Judy remarked.

'They're all the same round here,' and Olivia discovered that she had looked over her shoulder at the dark window behind.

'A Mrs Elizabeth Drew rents this house where Rita lived,' they were told as the camera returned to the door, 'so her assistance could be crucial in the search for Rita.' Just short of being subliminal, RECONSTRUCTION winked on the door as it opened. 'Mrs Drew was seen leaving the house two weeks ago but has not yet returned.'

Olivia came through the door, pulled it closed, checked the lock, walked down the path and round the gate. For a second there was a close-up of the gate swinging home, then a cut to Alan, head raised at the sound, and the camera went back to Olivia hurrying away up the street.

'That was masterly,' Judy congratulated. 'Rather like ghost writing. What shall we call it? Unrecognizable acting?'

'Perfected by an unrecognized actress. I warned you.'

'But I didn't believe you could do it.'

Laughing, they watched Alan shake his head, feel a pocket in his dungarees, walk to the back of the van and accept a cigarette from his mate.

'Nothing unrecognizable about that!' Judy whistled. 'He must have got wind of a new trophy: Walk On Actor of the Year. Let's see him again.'

On the second repeat they played it with him; on the third they imitated; by the time they came to the fifth they were taking him off. Their heads snapped up with cartoon suddenness, their eyes widened in pantomime astonishment, their hands squeezed pockets in a burlesque of frustrated search, their fingers grabbed at the proffered cigarette and cupped the match against gales in a parody of nicotine dependence, and they savoured its taste with the critical deliberation of connoisseurs testing a new brand.

While the video-recorder continued with the next programme, the 'Mystery of the Week' past, a mere sequence of pictures, touching or pretentious but inconsequential, their brief impact dissolved by the satire and fun.

'I've a feeling that wasn't quite admissible,' Judy said as they flopped on to the sofa; 'bitching my boyfriend.'

'I thought you'd forgotten.'

'Momentarily.' Judy frowned. 'I hope I was going for the actor, not the man.'

'Is there any difference?'

'Not a lot, but that doesn't worry me.' She shrugged, amused at herself. 'I think he'll relax when he gets work again. Without it, he has to keep reminding himself he's an actor. You're different.'

'Yes. As far as I'm concerned, I'm an actress only when I'm in work.'

'And a good one, Olivia. You'll lose confidence in yourself if you talk like that. You've a profession; it's simply that at the moment you're not engaged in it.'

Olivia nodded, wondering why Judy had chosen to ignore her meaning: that she separated the fictions of theatrical life from the actuality of the everyday.

Which was disrupted by knocking on the front door.

'That'll be him,' Judy said. 'Hell. He'll have your Mrs Winterton complaining if he goes on like that.'

15

'He won't. She's partisan, and in any case she's away for the week-end. I'm by myself.'

'Sad how years in bed-sits condition you to fear the wrath of landladies,' but she was at the window, peering up the dank shaft, shouting to Alan that she had heard and was on her way, then rushing round the room, picking up handbag, coat, looking for shoes, transforming their quiet into a rattle of departure.

To delay it, Olivia asked, 'Won't he come in for a cup of coffee?'

Shod, one arm sleeved, the other holding back the door, Judy paused. 'He anticipated that and said not. He wants to get straight back to his place. I've only twenty-four hours and he's piqued already by my spending four of them with you. It's worse than if you were a man.'

'Well, thank-you-Alan. But you don't have to humour him.'

'By galloping off? I haven't seen him, either, for five weeks. This isn't humouring Alan, darling; it's lust.'

Outside she crouched on the steps, dangled a hand at the cellar window and shouted, 'Before I depart, I'll give you a ring.'

'Do that. I'm never far from the phone.'

She was the width of her room away, plus twelve rises of cold stone and a causey of warped linoleum, when it sounded. Her sleep ruptured, wisps of dreams still clinging like the warmth of her bed, she rose, passed through the angling light, up a dark tunnel and into the bleached hall. Fuddled, stumbling towards the imperious phone, she felt the moon's presence, flinched at its glitter stinging her eyes, at its shaft pricking her nakedness and, as her hand reached out, she recoiled from its touch stained by its reach through the door's coloured glass and blotching her flesh.

She recited the number and waited. 'That you, Judy?' she asked and, more alert now, wondered at the hour.

'Judy, this is a damned silly time to call.' But already she knew that it was not Judy who had called her.

She waited, hearing nothing in the silent house but her own breaths and the contrapuntal echo against her ear. She waited, shivering under the moon's thrust, and saw transfixed upon the wall the silhouette of her breasts.

For some minutes she stood there, then she lowered the handset. In place again, it had a curious sheen in the moonlight. Because its waist was girdled with sweat.

Chapter Two

It was not until she had removed the sheet from her face and found that the morning's unaccustomed light came from the bedside lamp that Olivia remembered. She had been grateful for the lamp. Once such a light had corralled her against the night ogres of childhood; last night it had blunted the moon's edge and muted the hustling silence of the wire. The action, Olivia told herself, of a pervert flipping through the directory for women listed, dialling and listening, getting a thrill from the alarm in the voice and flesh goose-pimpling under a diaphanous night-gown. The absence of the latter she might mention, if he phoned again; the knowledge would drive him mad. On the other hand, his particular fetish might be of the Mrs Winterton variety, combinations under layers of winceyette. Olivia was pleased that she had not been bothered, but had to admit that, toughened by the bombardment of seventy years, Mrs Winterton might have found the call distressing only because she was denied stuffing her brolly down the man's throat. In her middle years a vigorous and probably just magistrate, she had a direct approach to punishment coupled with a militant defence of citizens' rights. Aspiring muggers fled from her path.

'He caught up with me on my left and began pulling at my handbag,' she had recounted to Olivia, 'but I was carrying my umbrella in my right hand so I swung round and jabbed him in the chest. He didn't like that, the scoundrel, and whined that he was only trying to attract my attention. Such boldness! I pointed out that he'd succeeded and would attract more if he didn't make himself scarce. It is advisable to act promptly and decisively, Olivia; in a tight spot one doesn't waste time asking questions.' Whereas Olivia would have liked to think that she might.

Deflected by the serried roofs, a halting peal of bells summoned the devout. There was no scurry of answering feet outside, but Olivia drew herself higher in the bed, stood a pillow against the headboard and leant upon it in saving pretence that soon she would get up. Such lassitude, with its laboured deceptions, was the main symptom of 'resting', the word which her mother had trilled so gaily, shying away from the question: resting from what or what for. Neither did she think herself inconsistent when she deplored the insecurity of the theatre yet used the gentle and protective euphemism that no other profession had coined. She might even have convinced herself, Olivia thought, that 'resting' was a kind of convalescence from work, while to Olivia and her colleagues it was the other way round.

Watching a blackbird pecking for worms five feet above her, Olivia considered how to occupy the day and decided wryly that, unlike the enviable employed, she could not justify it as one for leisurely recuperation. Many alternatives were closed to her, however: the Monday excitement of reading the Sunday papers in the library; the Wednesday run-through of her latest choreography for trolley and Muzak in the supermarket; the treat in collecting supplementary benefit; the invigorating walk round the museum, a way of keeping fit whatever the weather; the drama of the shift at the actors' agency, soliciting theatres, submitting photographs, checking availability, welcoming a call for a member to join a queue of fifty for an audition, suppressing the old theatrical chestnut, 'Whom do I have to sleep with to get the part?'

In a minute or two she would rise, wash in the

19

bathroom and dress. Perhaps she should dress first and stoke up the boiler; senile, and low-pulsed despite Mrs Winterton's brisk ministrations, it had probably taken the opportunity to expire in her absence. Resurrection would be sluggish; it could take all morning, after which there might be a few grudging pints of lukewarm water for washing up the previous night's pots. She ought also to wash the yellow sweat-shirt she had worn yesterday evening. There was still a smudge of grease on the sleeve where it had rubbed against the gate, for the cameraman, no doubt flouting union rules, had been liberal with oil to make the hinge move smoothly. The result was a mark on a garment that was almost a second skin. 'Not that again!' Judy had said.

After that, tidying her room, reading, preparing a meal, she would give the day a busyness though prompted by neither interest nor appetite; she would try to ignore that the busyness was artificial, that the difference between a day spent supine in bed and one spent supinely was merely a gesture at activity, feeble and tweaked.

The weeks had no urgency or distinction, the days level without perspective when she was not in a play. Rehearsals and performances did not reduce vitality but increased it, so that then every hour was crammed. Blithe, improvident with pleasures, she would entertain after shows, read until dawn, swim before perform-ances, and bring a sprightly efficiency to mundane tasks. The days had a wholeness then, and so had she. But when there was no work, neither she nor they had sub-stance; she was not entire. It was as if, by working on a part and projecting a character, she discovered her own, what she was capable of, or in what ways she was inad-equate. It was a chastening process at times, but always valuable.

Whatever occupation she contrived while she was 'resting', she felt empty. A cipher.

20

Judy's word. To describe the first part she'd had for six months. Except that it wasn't a part and had provided no stimulus because it had not engaged her. The demands of the programme had prevented that. There had been no text to work on, no situation, no clothes; not even a false eyelash or a touch of blonde rinse. Idly Olivia wondered what she would have done had more been required of her; built on observations of people who knew the woman, she supposed. There must be plenty in the town; the casting director must have found someone with a photograph or able to match Olivia's with the remembered face. The research might have been quite enjoyable, she reflected, slipping out of bed at the thought, like collecting material for an improvised play. Had she been offered more scope, she could have created an interesting role for herself, enough for someone to notice.

'Excuse me,' he began, a finger plucking the newspaper under her elbow.

She pushed the *Sunday Times* across the library table while she turned to the next page of advertisements in *Stage*.

Again the finger approached. It tapped. Olivia looked up.

He examined her face swiftly, the frame of her hair, then blushing, fixed his eyes on the neutral Formica between them. 'I'm sorry to interrupt but I had to speak,' breathless. 'I thought it was you. I saw you on television on Saturday.'

Her first fan! Brown eyes slightly bloodshot, off-white complexion, lantern jaw flecked by clumsy shaving, but transforming the dim lamp above her into a sun making vibrant the drab, patting her shoulders with restoring compliment. The dismissive attitude she had adopted with her mother had no place here.

'Kind of you to mention it,' she said, but it was inadequate appreciation for what he had done for her day.

Shy, as if unprepared for her warmth, he stared down at the table. 'You won't remember me, I suppose.'

He must have been among the clutch of bystanders who had watched, well away from the film unit and outside its magic ring.

'No; I'm afraid I don't. I hadn't much time.'

He nodded. 'That's right. You were generally busy.' Then, in a rush to articulate sentences which might disappear with the courage he had temporarily coerced: 'I didn't visit her often, in any case. Not many did. That's why I'm pleased you're back. Rita's missing, you see. My reason for approaching you like this. They thought you might be able to help.'

Astonished, Olivia felt like an actor wrongly addressed when coming on stage and who has to improvise a correction on behalf of the character not present.

'You've made a mistake. I'm not Elizabeth Drew. What you saw was a reconstruction.'

Somewhere in a back room a librarian keen on economy switched off the lights.

His diffidence was aggravated by her words but with an effort peering, 'You're right,' he stuttered.

'Absolutely. Inside information.'

For a moment he remained sober, then grinned. 'You must think me a fool.'

'Don't push me.'

'No, better not; but I am. Watching the programme, I knew it was a reconstruction, then when I saw you, I thought, She's come back. But by the time I introduced myself I was thinking it was her I'd seen on the box. I can't understand it.'

'You haven't introduced yourself.'

'Stephen Crayshaw. Steve.'

'I'm Olivia Quinn. Am I really so like her?'

He hesitated. 'I ought to say, yes. The features, shape,

colouring – they are all practically identical; but then, as soon as you speak, there's a difference. The vivacity changes everything.'

Through a window she saw the sun glint round a chimney, ready to light up the vivacity. She smiled.

'In that case, I'll have to keep talking.'

'It's true. I wasn't making a pass.'

'I know, but do carry on. Reconciling oneself to flattery is part of the job.'

Embarrassed, he muttered, 'I suppose so.'

To return to *Stage* now would be uncivil; she felt obliged to restore his brief ease. Casting round for a subject for chat, she could think of only one. 'How well do you know her?'

'Mrs Drew? Hardly at all. I can't remember ever speaking to her. She'd be about, but I didn't really want to get into conversation with her. It was Rita I was visiting so I tended to just slide by.'

He looked a natural for sliding by. Olivia's lips twitched. 'Like that, was it?'

'Not really,' he corrected. 'She wasn't the sort of landlady who lurks but I don't think she was overfond of men.'

He seemed an undeserved target for dislike. 'Well, you've managed to speak to her this morning – I'll be as bad as you soon – to her proxy, I should say.'

They laughed. 'Because I'm worried about Rita. I haven't seen her for some weeks, then suddenly there was her photograph on television. It was eerie, like seeing a ghost. I keep telling myself that they are making a lot of nothing; Rita never stays long in one place. But I can't forget that room. I had to switch off. Luckily you came on before I got to the button.'

She wondered why he considered her appearance to be lucky. 'I know nothing more than you.'

'You didn't pick up any theories?'

'They weren't interested in theories; that's for the police, and I was just doing a job: two hours' messing about and thirty seconds of filming. I wasn't included in any discussions, if there were any. I simply did as I was instructed, and as far as the acting went I could have been part of the set.'

'You did fine! Except that I can't imagine Mrs Drew banging a gate. They got that wrong. I think they got something else wrong, too. There was something wrong about the room, but I can't work out what it was. Of course, it's a bit since I was in it so the memory's blurred. The cutting didn't help, either. You were never given an overall view, just details in close-up. It was sickening.'

'Yes.'

They were silent, thinking of the scene.

'I suppose we have to accept that kind of obscenity,' he concluded. 'If something has happened to Rita, then that programme can only do good. People will be keeping their eyes open, looking out for her. I thought of looking, but where? If there's anything you can do, you will, won't you?'

Surprised, she raised a shoulder in negligent assent. 'Of course, but I can't imagine what. I don't know this place or anyone who lives here. At present it's convenient for me to be near my agency; it's a co-operative and we run it in shifts, so it's easier to lodge in the district. When you have work, of course, you move where it is. A case of: have Equity card, will travel.'

He nodded, sympathetic. 'For your sake, then, I hope you move soon.'

Had he been someone from the agency she would have asked, flirtatious, for whose sake would she *not* move soon. To Stephen, however, she murmured acknowledgement and waved to his, 'All the best, then,' as he left her, a strange young man, bashful yet steady, nervous yet firm in condemnation of the programme. It was odd that, clearly no cretin, he should have addressed her as Mrs Drew. Perhaps, tuned to the chance of meeting someone who might help him find

Rita, he had allowed anxiety to translate hope into belief.

She could hear it ringing as she walked up the street and her neck was greased by memories of Sunday bells chiming through the silence of the lifted phone. Repeated and repeated. So she pretended it belonged to a neighbour and lingered by the gate feeling for her key, sure of its place yet letting her fingers prolong the search. But like a petulant child demanding attention the ringing continued then, the door tardily opened, it ceased as she entered the hall.

On the ebb of its sound Mrs Winterton shouted from the kitchen, 'If they would wait, I could lay my hands on it. They stop the minute I get close.'

Along the linoleum footprints in mud indicated how far she had come to proximity. She followed them. Feeling the squeeze of clay under a boot, she bent down, peeled off the lump and dropped it into her pocket. The action was not occasioned by a fleeting interest in cleanliness, Olivia decided, but by a reverence befitting the substance from which they were both derived.

'I'm out at the back,' Mrs Winterton explained and added impishly, 'tilling.'

As usual charmed, Olivia smiled back. 'A pity you haven't more to till.' Six feet of soggy clods under a verdigris elder.

'No. I'm a realist. My ambitions are modest. I wouldn't ask for any more.'

'Did you have a good week-end?'

'A week-end, Olivia, is never good with my sister Dorothy. It is spent listening to tales of woe. In middle age she looked forward to her declining years in the expectation of being cosseted by her adoring husband. Unfortunately he displayed a singular selfishness and died before taking up duty. So she is left to nurse her hypochondria alone and I'm afraid that she hasn't the stamina for it. She has, however, a television set which she calls her life-support machine. In that case, I told her, we must equip her with an alternative in the event of a power cut, and switched it off. The alternative was not the peace I had hoped for; depressing one button merely released another. Dorothy talked all week-end, without ceasing and with a good deal of repetition. With the result that I may consider obtaining a contraption against her next visit. It would stem the flow and allow me to nod off. All this, Olivia, is not to demonstrate that Dorothy's loquacity is contagious but to explain why, though in the presence of a television set, I did not see your brief appearance. How did it look?'

'Adequate, I'd say; which was all I could aim for. It won't bring a job.'

'I suppose not, but you can't be sure. It might bear fruit; large oaks from little acorns grow. Looking back, I'm surprised how often the important things in my life have arisen by accident from what seemed an insignificant event.'

Olivia nodded, aware that she had been contemptuous of similar sentiments expressed by her mother.

'So you mustn't grow down-hearted, Olivia. It may be that being on television has had an effect because people have been clamouring for you all morning. There have been at least five calls,' charitably discounting that any could have been intended for her. 'When you ring your agency, would you please ask them to be a little more patient? Tell them that, if I'm answering the phone, they have to allow for the halt, lame and blind. Being of the theatre, they will be able to imagine that.'

Watching her return to the kitchen, noticing how she fitted her boots into the prints of clay like a child who avoids cracks in the pavement, Olivia reminded herself that the calls might have come from the agency as Mrs Winterton had assumed.

'Yes, we have tried to get you,' Earl answered. 'There's

been an availability check for the Piccolo Theatre for July. I said I'd have to find out whether you are free; that was in order to introduce a hint of healthy competition. They're auditioning in London the end of this week. Will let us know by tomorrow if you're called. I decided it was in nobody's interest to quibble about the short notice, or to ask why they couldn't arrange an audition straight off. She was obviously some timorous little mouse delegated to flick through the files and come up with a list for the director to stab his pin into.'

'What's the play?'

'Sorry; I didn't ask. Miniature, I expect, since it has to fit in that theatre.'

'I don't know it.'

'Neither do I. Another joke belly-flops into the sewer.'

'Oh, I see. Sorry.'

'I can take it, dear, wiping the egg yolk off his face. You're rather short on enthusiasm, Olivia. I know this check isn't the most marvellous thing that could happen, but it's better than nothing.'

'Yes.'

'Feeling neglected?'

Mrs Winterton had said that the telephone had rung five times. 'A bit.'

'My shoulder's free for crying upon.'

'Thanks, Earl.'

'Good. Unfortunately I'm playing squash tonight but do you fancy tomorrow? If you starve till then you might be able to face one of Greasy Len's hamburgers.'

'All right. I'll slot it into my appointments diary. Earl, did you call me about anything else? I've been at the library and my landlady was out in the back yard. The person always rang off before she could reach the phone.'

'We'll have to remember that. Yes, I have another item to report, ma'am, clicking his heels. It's rather odd. The parents of that girl who's missing have been on asking if they could have your number. They were given this one by Pennine News. I didn't know what the policy is on that, but Alan had popped in – our very own strong, decisive though slightly muscle-bound Alan after a day with the nubile Judy – and he whispered instructions. So I didn't give them your number but agreed to pass on a message. They're anxious to speak to you. How's it feel to be an instant celebrity?'

'Not so hot. Why should they want to speak to me?'

'I don't know; they didn't say. More precisely, the father didn't. It was him on the line, and a man of few words, somewhat uptight. Not one to give much away.'

'I don't feel like ringing him.'

'You can't do that, anyway. He only left the address: 24 Cattlegate, near the glue factory, which figures.'

'Does that mean that he is asking me to visit them? I can't possibly. What would be the use?' Stephen had said, If there's anything you can do, you will, won't you?

'*Use*? How do you mean, use? I assumed that he wished to thank you for taking part in the film.'

'That wasn't to do him a favour. And he could have said that to you, couldn't he? I've no wish to go round and collect.' Her voice had leapt higher, tight with control.

'Now careful, love; it's not a summons from Peter Hall. Ignore it. I told him it was unlikely that you'd have the time.'

That really was a joke. 'Thanks, Earl,' she said, but without bitterness.

'All part of the service: protecting our stars from the public. Only please don't do the same for me some time.'

'I promise. Has anything else come through?'

'Isn't that enough for one morning? Must return to the typewriter. Be with you tomorrow evening. About eight?'

'Yes.' If Earl had tried to speak to her only twice, then the caller's total had reached yesterday morning's figure, but she could not ask him to recall the number of attempts he had made. The request would oblige her to give reasons for it and she would not be able to conceal her conviction that she was the person's deliberate choice. She did not wish to hear herself say that. Describing the silence on the telephone, giving it an intention, would grant it, like a character on stage, a definite substance; it would be fleshed out, truly exist.

'Look, Olivia,' his voice was saying, 'I wish you'd co-operate. I'm trying to put this down but I can hear you thinking. On the count of three, girl, will you please replace the handset. And forget the father. He must be going frantic, I imagine, but that doesn't oblige you to sit and hold his hand. It's not as if "Mystery of the Week" is a popular series and you have to be nice to the fans. In the circumstances, I should ignore it. Curtain. One, two . . .'

The circumstances were a girl disappeared and a father going frantic.

Cattlegate was a street of corroded houses, windows nailed close against the rattling gusts and the stench of the factory behind. Doors, their thresholds elevated by precipitous steps, opened straight on to the pavement divided into unstaked but confidently held strips in which were set a pram or a tricycle, a plastic rack for milk bottles, a wheelchair, boot scrapers or tubs sprouting flowers. Number 24 had a window-box screwed to its sill and an iron handrail to assist the feeble up the two steps. Olivia held it as she listened to the movements startled by her knock. The door opened, offering a stripe of face.

Across the anchoring chain Olivia said, 'I understand that you've been trying to get in touch with me. I'm from On Cue – the actors' agency. Olivia Quinn.'

The woman frowned. 'Oh, yes. I thought for a minute it was her. I've been hoping ever since that programme, but nothing's come of it. He's in the bathroom.' Her gaze lifted over the other's shoulder and her lips puckered as if she were trying to work out what she should do.

Embarrassed, Olivia considered offering to visit again later, and not go back, but the woman recalled civility and began fiddling with the chain.

'You'd better come in. I'll go and fetch.'

The room was the 'best' one, the show-piece for strangers, preserved in polish and sealed from the odours and steam of the kitchen at its back. The arms of the three-piece suite were covered in sleeves which, matching the upholstery, camouflaged the wear, and the empty grate had been stuffed with paper then concealed by a screen. A plastic vase containing artificial flowers stood on the sideboard between two photographs: Mrs Dale younger, shivering under scarves, one hand clutching a bouquet and the other hooked through the arm of a man already balding who had raised his chin to receive the camera, and was sombre and stiff; the other photograph was of an earlier period and a different man. Dressed in the uniform of the Royal Artillery, he lounged on a bench outside a pub and his dishevelled hair, his hand flourishing a bottle and his laughter were the only source of vivacity and spontaneous enjoyment in that circumspect room.

'Reginald Dale,' the first man introduced himself, pushing his wife in front of him and proffering his hand. 'Please sit down.'

They sat opposite each other, separated by the screened hearth. Mrs Dale stood by the window and twitched the curtains, snagging the net. His glance moved her to a straight-backed chair by the door and she sat tensely like someone waiting to be summoned.

'She's not herself at the moment,' he said. 'She's very upset. You must excuse her. No one cared for a daughter more than Mrs Dale.'

There was a sniff from the chair. Olivia dared not look.

'She'll pull herself together, given a bit of time. It's no

good pining. Better to square up, occupy herself, not moon about waiting for news. It could be weeks before that comes, if it ever does, and she must prepare herself for the worst. That's sensible.'

Horror dried her mouth; her breath stopped. Sensible to anticipate Rita's death. That's what he's saying, Olivia told herself, and aloud managed: 'She'll turn up.' But, coming in a whisper, the words confirmed his and drifted across the room tidied for mourners.

'If she does, then we shall be the more thankful. But it's wise not to rely on it. We know what that can lead to.' His eyes were on Olivia but she knew he was addressing his wife. Finished, he looked quickly towards the straight-backed chair, his expression a warning.

She wanted to get away. She couldn't think why she had come. She had expected anxiety, not this resolute denial of life. It was grotesque and chilling.

'I must go,' she said.

'The young man in the office said you were busy.'

She waited, giving him time to explain why he had wished to meet her. Soot in a damp flurry grazed down the wad of paper and splattered over the hearth.

'It's raining,' he said. 'I'll get an umbrella.'

He had gone before she could prevent him. Standing by the door, she had to speak to the wife. 'I'm sorry about Rita.'

'You're an actress, aren't you? Rita always says she doesn't know how they can do it, up on a stage.'

After the man's conviction, the change of tense was shocking; it was like the resuscitation of a corpse. Grasping the knob, Olivia tugged at the door but it was damp and would not budge.

'She can have her room again any time,' Mrs Dale went on, her voice almost inaudible as if engaged in a private chant. 'The bed's always made, she knows that, I've told her often enough. There's no need for her to

31

go elsewhere. Nobody can replace a mother.' The final sentence was an appeal.

Mesmerized, Olivia found herself shaking her head.

'Of course not,' the other agreed, satisfied. 'You're supposed to look like her, aren't you? I wouldn't know about that but I can tell that's as far as it goes. You wouldn't do it, but we can comfort ourselves that in the end folk get their deserts. All the same, I have to admit that Rita is very impressionable.' She faltered at the last word, rolling it in her mouth as if practising a new description.

It was meaningless raving but Olivia could not stammer out palliatives; they were stopped by 'get their deserts' and the accompanying malice in the woman's face. She pulled at the door.

'I've found you an umbrella,' the man said over her shoulder. 'There's no need to return it. Mother and me have got ours.'

She was trapped. She couldn't get out. She was in a set where all the doors were locked and, with lines used up and role completed, she was forced to continue the scene.

'I'll manage, thank you.'

'It's a bit on the common side, to my way of thinking, but it's in good condition, almost brand-new,' and he opened the umbrella out. The flare of scarlet dotted with yellow trefoils challenged the room. 'I'd like you to have it.'

Unable to escape, she turned, saw the pleading and, no longer practical, the uncovered grief.

'It belonged to Rita.'

And she recalled from a decade earlier a friend's death and she, not yet eleven, sent to visit at the mother's request. They had sat without speaking; there was nothing to say. Until finally the woman had given her a ring. 'You recognize it? I'd like you to have it. Now you may go.' It was as though Olivia's visit had brought her for the last time near the dead girl and, seeing this other to the door, stroking her arm with an absorbed obsequial gesture, she had bad her daughter farewell.

'Thank you,' Olivia said.

But out of the house, with another street between them, Olivia let down the umbrella she had obediently unfurled and allowed the rain to wipe across her face. For she had not been Rita's friend; she had never known her, their only connection a woman Olivia resembled and had represented in a two-minute film. She had never met this girl whose father was prepared for her death. That was preposterous; there was no suspicion, no hint.

The rain was coming faster. It bounced on her cheeks, filled her hair and washed along her throat. Vigorous, assertive, it repulsed the joyless sepulchral place she had just left and drew a response from her flesh. Then she was running, running as she had that day from Pam's mother, feeling the spring of muscles, knowing the race of blood, assured by the pumps of her breath; because she was alive, licked by the rain, flushed by the swirling air, her feet gliding over tarmac and her eyes brushing colour over the damp sepia streets.

She ran without slackening, given over to sensation, unimpeded by Rita's umbrella wedged in the crook of her arm, oblivious of strollers and shoppers and school-children. And taking vitality from the rain and combing draughts, she was surprised and elated by a purpose which began to flicker in her mind.

So she had reached the door of her lodgings and had inserted the key before she heard the car. Without turning her head she listened to it idle for a second then pass on.

Chapter Three

'You're crackers!' From anyone else, the sentence would have expressed astonishment or disapproval. Alan made it into a statement of fact.

'Gives me something to do.'

'So would bug hunting.'

She could not understand why Judy went for him. It could only be his beautiful body – alleged. Had she known it was Alan she was speaking to she would not have mentioned it; but when she came in from her search Mrs Winterton had been holding the telephone, and her greeting, 'It's that nice young man from the agency' had been such a relief that she had rushed straight in with: 'Earl, remember that Rita Dale? Well, I've begun to look for her.' She had forgotten it was another day, Alan on rota.

'With about as much sense,' he added.

'Perhaps I'm not sensible.' Not in the way the father suggested. 'Any news your end?'

'Have you really blown your mind? This is an actors' co-operative, not a bloody detective agency.'

She grinned at the misunderstanding. 'A brilliant deduction, my dear Watson. I was thinking along those lines myself. Heard from the Piccolo?'

'Not yet; but if nothing comes through by five I'm going to give them a ring. They should have let us know before now if they want to see you on Saturday, which is a bloody silly day to audition anyway. Apparently the director's in Edinburgh the beginning of this week, so he can't start auditions till Thursday.

Anybody would think actors don't qualify for a week-end's leisure.' As if many of them would not have enjoyed that all week! 'They should have phoned earlier. It's Tuesday, for God's sake.' Alan the high-powered tycoon. She wondered whether the City were conscious of its loss.

'I think they'll have a calendar, Alan.' When he tele-phoned them, however, he would make a switch. She had heard him: cool, businesslike and discreetly flatter-ing, practising his young but immensely experienced civil servant, executive grade. 'All the same, I'd be glad to know, but their silence almost certainly means that they have decided not to call me.' She felt less forlorn than usual. Six months' disappointments must have anaesthetized the nerves.

'That's no excuse.' He paused. Olivia sighed. Some crummy director had once told him to count out his pauses and she could hear him now – on his fingers. 'Heard anything from Judy?' he finally enunciated his line.

'No. It was only Saturday that she was here.' She would have liked to add, 'Remember?' Alan was the sort of man you were under contract to provoke.

'I thought you two were in touch. Constantly.'

'You know, Alan, there are two large panes of clear glass in this front door. They aren't as nice as the leaded lights that fell out but they do allow an uninterrupted view of the hall where I'm standing.'

'What?'

'So all you have to do is run over, take a peek and check.'

'You don't have to be offensive. All I asked was . . .'

'Whether I'd heard from Judy and the answer was, no. That didn't merit a sarcastic comment.'

'You're being very touchy, Olivia. Sorry I inquired. All I wanted to know was whether she had got back to base safely and you are the obvious person to ask.' The waspish tone had been smothered in diplomatic urbanity. 'When she rings you, would you mind asking her to telephone me?'

'I don't expect she'll ring. It's a busy week. You know very well that it's her first night on Thursday. Anyway, she's on the phone.'

'Yes, technically. The theatre doesn't like private calls, however, and she was in the bath or something when I rang her place last night. Also this morning. Very devoted to personal hygiene, at the moment, is Judy.' The laugh was forced.

'You're not telling me you've had a row?'

'You'd like that, dear, wouldn't you? But don't waste your powers of detection on us. You'll need them all for little Rita Dale, God help her,' and the handset clattered down.

Judy had said that he had been cross because she wouldn't go straight to his digs on Saturday; now that for some reason she was avoiding him, he was venting his frustration upon Olivia. He was blaming their friendship and suggesting that she desired the undivided attachment that he claimed for himself. Still holding the telephone, Olivia felt his spite stitch along her arm as the wire burred on, not silent but, again, wordless. When she replaced the handset she found it necessary to wipe it upon her sleeve.

Down in her room she hung up her jacket, stood Rita's umbrella in a basin to drip, and made herself a cup of tea. By these small unremarkable tasks normality was resumed, and sitting under the submerged window with its ragged canopy of weeds, she considered the day. It had begun well, pulling her out of bed by the skid of the paper boy's boots, whisking her into the bathroom with a teasing intention, rinsing sleep from her eyes with the reminder of what that was. It had not mattered that she had no idea how to carry it out. It had not mattered that the light, rusted by rain, dropped into the basement and dulled her clothes' individuality and colour as she dressed. It had not mattered that she could not brush off the mud from her denims still damp from the previous day or that her trainers remained sodden and she had to go out in pumps. It had not mattered that the task seemed impossible, that the inquiries which now occurred to her: at bus station, Job Centre, to neighbours, would already have been made. All that mattered was that she leave her basement room, climb up into this town which she had never bothered to explore or be more than casually acquainted with, and begin her search.

And unbelievably, not expecting a reward, she had received one.

Approaching the bus station and trying to calculate how long it would take to speak to every driver – number of drivers employed (unknown) times frequency of shifts – she heard the rap of stiletto heels behind her and a panted, 'Hi!'

Olivia turned to a girl who, blushing, dropped the hand outstretched to detain her. 'Sorry,' she said and made to pass on. 'I thought you were a friend.'

Another mistaken recognition. 'Do I resemble her from behind as well?' she demanded.

Halted by Olivia's astonishment, the other echoed, '*As well*? You aren't like her at all. I wouldn't have thought anything about the pumps and denims – hers are generally mucky – if it hadn't been for the umbrella.'

'It isn't mine. Wait a second.' She had to adjust. 'Look, are we talking about Rita Dale?'

'Who else do you think you might look like from behind? You a friend of hers, too?'

'I haven't met her, but I was lent this umbrella. Do you know that she's missing?'

'Do you mean missing proper or just bunked off?'

'I'm not sure. I want to find out.'

'Why're you so interested? You're not from the DHSS, are you?'

'No. I've never been invited across the counter.'

The girl smiled. 'You sound like Rita. I don't see how you've got her umbrella if you don't know her.'

Karen herself did not know Rita well; their acquaintance was limited to random meetings in a pub: 'You know how it is, recognize a face you remember from school and you wave and maybe have a quick chat if there's nothing else doing.' This casualness had affected their conversation; interrupted by pedestrians weaving round them, abbreviated by Karen's need not to miss a bus, it was disconnected and superficial. Under the sheltering umbrella, recollections would begin strongly then drift, refracted by the rain. Accustomed to seeking even in the most circuitous dialogue the movement towards its goal, Olivia, as she sat in her room and squinted up the dim shaft, tried to give their talk coherence.

Rita always seemed happy enough and the mention of Stephen had brought a laugh: he was one of God's own worriers. As far as Karen knew, he'd never been Rita's boyfriend, not properly, and she didn't need him to fuss. Karen reckoned she was all right now. The question, 'Now?' had been answered by a tart, 'She's got her own place, hasn't she?' followed by wariness. Karen didn't like to say, but she reckoned there might have been some bother. Rita was upset one night and got drunk. No, she didn't know anything about the state the house had been left in, sharply reminding Olivia that she hadn't watched 'Mystery of the Week'. 'Do me a favour! It's the disco down at the Palace on Saturday nights. You took off her landlady, did you? So why're you asking me?'

This latter question was repeated at the Job Centre, an assistant inquiring suspiciously why, if Olivia wanted to know what her friend was up to, she didn't ask her herself; and bus drivers, bolting for cover in the form of a tea break, mumbled, 'Never look at a face, love; I've got enough on my plate watching the traffic and seeing to tickets. The inspector's your man.' Who said, after two hours' invigorating warm-up jumping the routes, 'Your best bet is to ask your friend's mum, love. She'd know.'

'Why didn't you say you were a journalist?' Earl asked as they waited for Len to grease a hamburger. 'People love to think they're going to be in a story. They'd have talked, whether they knew anything or not.'

'No doubt. But fantasies won't solve the problem.'

'Not solve it, no; but they might by chance give you a line as you sift through. It's not so far from the way we work sometimes, is it? Particularly if there's not much in the part. We find a possibility and fill it out. Some even start from the clothes. God knows what they do if they're playing Adam.'

She laughed. He had not said she was crackers. 'I'm after a situation, not a character, Earl, and I'm not playing one, either. As a matter of fact, that's why I didn't pretend to be a journalist; I did consider it. But somehow I didn't feel the part.'

Earl rolled his eyes and took another sip of his beer. 'Olivia, you don't have to *feel* a journalist when all you have to do is ask a few questions. "Good afternoon. Would you mind giving me a moment? I'm from the *Gossip* and I'm investigating the disappearance of a young woman from a house in Hackney Street. I should like to ask you a few questions. You'll find them absolutely painless and you don't have to bother about details such as fact and truth; I'll see to all that. You may remain perfectly anonymous if you prefer because that's at the discretion of the editor." If you *felt* it, Olivia, you'd be doing more than the journalists themselves.'

39

'Cynicism is not permitted. You're supposed to have a spontaneous, natural and trusting approach to life, remember. It was simply that I doubted whether I could do it, just cold, striding in, especially after yesterday.'

She had already told Earl of her visit to Cattlegate.

He winced. 'That was disgusting.'

'Yes, but . . . thinking about it, what Mr Dale said seems so bizarre that I can hardly believe I got it right. He did talk in exactly the way I've told you but it wasn't really to me but to his wife, as if he were telling her more than she must not rely on Rita's being found. And he was holding something back. That makes me wonder if he were trying to suggest something quite the opposite when he gave me the umbrella. Do you suppose he did in the hope that it might lead me to Rita? It's collected one friend, sort of, already.'

'That's too far-fetched. OK for a pot-boiling thriller to pull in the coachloads but people don't behave like that in real life. You didn't think that at the time.'

'Because it reminded me of Pam's mother.'

'Right, so trust your instincts. As I'm supposed to do.'
They grinned.

'All the same, I think I shall go back.'

'To that loony bin?'

'Ostensibly to return the umbrella, but I should be less agitated the second time; I shall be prepared. So I may be able to get the family line on Rita.'

'You might. And that's the right way to express it because their line won't be the only one.' He groaned, shading his eyes with a fist. 'Imagine what my lot wouldn't say about me!'

'That's if they knew it all. Loyalty would keep them quiet, wouldn't it? As it does my mother. In this case though, I might learn a lot from what they don't say.'

'But you won't find the girl that way, Olivia. As you've

said, you're after a situation and that's character stuff. Which could get at you. Sure you can cope?'

He was still puzzled by her inability to play a journalist. Soon he would make the connection. Quickly, because she was not ready for that, she evaded. 'Now who's going over the top? Anyway, tomorrow night I may find out where she is. I'm meeting some of her mates in a pub. Karen turned up again, mid-afternoon, leaping off a bus as I lay in wait for its driver. "That was a real crappy interview," she announced, " 'bout fitted the job, but I'll take it if offered. I'm sick of living like money had gone out of fashion, though why I sweated for five O levels just for packing boxes, you tell me. Him who saw me couldn't. But coming back, when I'd finished working out what would be left after my stamp and that, I had a think. About Rita. It's a bit of a mystery, in' it? I'll ask round. We'll be in the pub tomorrow night, the Gate, by the market. Come if you want. Might as well. You never know what you might pick up. Only not Wayne. He's mine." '

'Shall you go?'

'Yes.'

'I hate to sound discouraging, Olivia, but isn't this a job for the police?'

'I suppose it is, but they don't seem to have got very far, do they? They haven't been questioning Rita's friends. Karen didn't even know she had disappeared.'

'They may not consider there's a case to be investigated. That "Mystery of the Week" seems to have dealt with a totally spurious piece of news. If there were anything in it, the police would have started looking not only for Rita but for the landlady as well, and the Dales would have been told. They would have to have a reason for beginning a search, one that was worth the use of police time.'

'That's not a commodity I'm short of.'

'It's not the time you may spend on it that worries

me,' but he did not ask her to justify her decision. 'Len's signalling. No, you sit tight. I'll collect.'

The day's Hot Rod Hamburger came with lashings of diesel oil, a washer of carbonized onion and a mesh of burnt chips. Earl stripped his down with the tissue provided and added mustard to weaken the taste. 'I can't take it straight,' he told her. 'That would be flying in the face of nature.' The joke, however, was automatic to fill in a pause.

'You may ask me,' she said. After his patience it was unfair to hold out.

'Not if you don't wish. I'll just put it down to stage fright, off stage.'

'It was because I couldn't do it like that. It was too . . . artificial. It didn't fit.' The meat was tough; it had to be chewed so much it blocked off the breath. 'I couldn't frame the questions in a way a journalist would have done, with that kind of prodding inquisitiveness. I could only inquire as if I were a friend.' She had said it. She had admitted it to them both.

Earl made a pass at his hamburger, snapping chips. 'And you've never met her. Well, I'm hardly the one to comment on that. It's extraordinarily emotional but,' he shrugged, 'so be it.'

'I feel I must find her.'

'I hope not in order to contradict her father's ghoulish prediction.'

Earl is sharp, she thought; never misses a trick. 'No; at least, not entirely. That accentuated a feeling already there, though I had tried to dismiss it. Probably that's why I visited them. I can't account for this, but I feel committed, and not in a rational way. How's that for a piece of sloppy professionalism? Do wonders for my acting, this will, won't it?'

'Stop that, Olivia.'

'It's the whole thing: that memory of Pam, and the mother suddenly hissing that people get their deserts –

42

Heaven knows what she meant – and Alan bitching over Judy. They all have the same effect on me. It doesn't matter to me whether the police think there is a case to investigate, Earl. I can't pay attention to quibbles like that. Because I feel as if something very vulnerable and fragile is under attack and I must save it. I feel drawn in. Ever since making that film I've felt drawn in, though I pretended that I didn't. Two hours' work, Earl, the first time I've earned money in six months, and this is what it does to me!'

'Well, you might say, dear, you've got more than your money's worth. I've never been lucky enough to get a non-speaking part that gave me all this lovely passion, gratis,' playing camp. His facetiousness was deliberate and, because he was Earl, it did not pain her. The mask he had chosen had a chink; anxiety peeped through.

She nodded. 'I'll try,' meaning: try to steady up.

'Good.' He staked a chip on a tine of his fork and began carefully, 'Talking of films . . . Raymond came into the office yesterday and told me about that bit part he had with Granada. Would you like to hear? OK. It is rather choice. I told him it was absolutely made for his next circuit of the clubs, but he brushed that aside. Ever since Granada spotted him and gave him that small part as a bruiser, he's had the bug. As he confided, he wants to concentrate on going straight. Seems a perverse ambition for a stand-up comic, but there we are. All he had to do – one episode in the series – was walk up to a VIP who's just alighted from a train and say, "Welcome home, Fred." Fred being a local lad who's made good, is now an international name and is returning from some celebration, so he's being met by civic dignitaries, brass band, etc. Our Raymond, luckily without mayoral chains, is one of the welcoming party.

'The week before the take he assured wardrobe that

he had an appropriate suit, and the night before he went into training for stardom by limiting his ale intake to five pints and rejecting the overtures of his missis so that he was not, as he said, played out on the day. Isn't he gorgeous? The call was for nine o'clock on Huddersfield station. Arising in good time, he took down his suit on which he had not laid a hand since he got wed fourteen years ago. "But you've got a fifteen-year-old daughter," I protested. "She came a bit before," he defended. And before ale and laughs in working men's clubs. Because, as you will have guessed, the suit didn't fit. However, the trousers had been on the big side, so a discreet snip at the waistband sorted them out, and the jacket didn't look too bad if he left it unfastened. The waistcoat, though, was more problematic, but Raymond and Mrs Ray aren't a couple to be defeated by a four-inch gap. They simply transferred that to the back. She sliced up the back seam, he buttoned up the front and she stapled the open edges to his shirt. Thus costumed, Raymond sallied forth.

'It took him some time to get into Huddersfield station, of course. He hadn't reckoned with the amount of parking space a television unit takes up. Neither, I suppose, had the innocent public. In the end he slipped his car into a place reserved for the disabled and got past a policeman by dragging a paralysed leg. So he was only twenty minutes late. Fortunately the brass band were complaining about the acoustics, so nobody noticed. The rehearsal went perfectly. The fanfare started up; the home side shambled down the platform; the assistant director stepped down from a stationary train; Raymond moved forward, grasped his hand and bellowed his line. He did it to perfection, he told me. They were all over him. According to Raymond it is very unusual for anyone to sustain such a line without making a fault or even forgetting it. He

44

was insistent about that. Further rehearsal was deemed unnecessary and the cast was given an hour to cool down. Raymond managed to evade the close inspection of the wardrobe mistress by warning her that she'd provided the chap playing the mayor with the wrong sort of chain, signed three girls' autograph books in the name of Charles Bronson, borrowed a stapler from property, performed running repairs in the lavatory, joined the party in the snack bar and consumed six polythene beakers of British Rail tea. That was, sad to say, his undoing. Raymond was very insistent about that. When the gut's used to beer, it's dangerous to change. That can upset the chemical stability of the whole organism, in which generous bulk Raymond includes his head.

'The call came for the take; the sheet was removed from the red carpet; banners were dusted; the brass band negotiated a note; the welcoming party lined up; the director retreated; the cameramen adjusted their sights and the train inched into the station. Fred and his entourage had been put on at Leeds and though it was impossible to disguise their business from the legitimate passengers, they had been asked to ignore what was happening and to alight in their usual fashion from the train. It pulled up. The crucial coach was opposite the civic party. They slid forward. The door of the coach swung open. Raymond strode across, grabbed the chap's hand, pumped it heartily, leered into the camera and recited, "Welcome home, Fred." "I appreciate the thought, mate," the other answered, "but the name's Sam." '

It was many minutes before Earl could continue. His story relaxed tensions and their laughter was wild and anarchic. Customers glad of the respite from chewing turned in their chairs and stared. One shouted, 'Let's all share the joke.' Grateful, loving Earl for such restoration, Olivia put her arms round his shoulders and gently butted his head.

'So they had to take it again,' he concluded. 'They had to ferry Fred and his party back to Leeds and put him on another train; they had to keep the brass band on for another three hours; they had to pay the whole cast for another half-day. Must have cost a bomb. And do you know what Raymond said? That it was pretty good, having only the two takes, because some actors are so thick it's necessary to do it over and over again, whereas, come tea-time, they had finished. Unfortunately he didn't manage to get in a word about future engagements; the director was busy and kept waving him off but he's confident he'll get more. Apparently the casting secretary when approached admitted that she had liked the way he had moved. Incorrigibly.'

And they were shrieking again. Finally Olivia gasped, 'But Ray can't be serious?'

'That's the trouble. You're never quite sure whether he is or not. He went through all that with a completely straight face while I was creased up. So he's left us to think that he might really expect he'll get more work after that, just as he's left us undecided whether the joke is on him or on us. He ought to keep to the clubs; he's wasted anywhere else. Now I'm going to buy you another beer and then you're going to tell me what you've chosen to take for audition on Saturday.'

She had not yet decided; the call had reached her late that afternoon. Then, tired by her unsuccessful quest and trying to coerce a utility in Karen's invitation, she had been stirred to nothing more than a limp interest, inquiring about the London trains, ordering the ticket with the agency, repeating a routine which was as stale and dispirited as the hope. Earl had altered that; he had made her laugh; he had re-established a perspective in which the occurrences of the last three days shrank to a manageable size.

46

So now as she sat at the table, Earl waiting at the counter which Len called his bar, she anticipated with more enthusiasm the Saturday audition, its brief replication of an appearance on stage, and she felt the characteristic excitement which was a paradox of enjoyment and fear. The occasion became not a useless chore but a pleasure generous with promise, creating a condition in which both her own problem and that of Rita could be resolved. For the day's energy had been wrestled from the hold of her private dejection; now it sprang up without restraint, it rippled with optimism and sparkled her brain. As stretching back, she contemplated the audition, she was eager also to renew her search. No longer was she noosed by the father's behaviour. She was capable, ready; she winked across at Earl and smiled at the attentive customers. She no longer blanched at the memory of Alan's spite.

Neither did she blanch when the man caught her eye. He was sitting alone at a table, a large man, one hand clenched by the side of an empty plate. Unaccompanied, isolated from the talk and clatter, he swilled the beer round his glass then drank from it mechanically without removing his look from her face. And struck by his slumped loneliness, by his appearance of having been cast off, Olivia had smiled and nodded before she had registered the quality of his stare.

He was up immediately, the abrupt lunge causing the table to rock and his chair to sway then snap obediently straight at the thrust of a knee, which in a second had jabbed at a leg of the table she occupied, upon which were crunched two red, knuckled fists. Jerking back, Olivia heard the smack of her shoulder against the unplastered wall and saw his thrill at her pain. 'You bitch,' he sneered.

She was aware of silence and halted movement, of a film stopped and holding postures incomplete which gradually uncoiled as the reel resumed, bringing people towards them but slowly, languorously, arms outstretched but floating, delicate in a mockery of haste. While gasses of grease and beer smothered, adding the words: 'Filthy cow' and '. . . tell us what they do.' Then the fists scraped back, the face shot up, the chest was hooped in ridged arms and Len was whispering, 'Right, mate, the door's open. When I put you down, you're out of here in one second flat,' followed by curses, the scratch of shoes on tiles, the crash of stools, the thud of a slammed door, Len's face telling her the man had been seen to, Earl holding her hand, murmurs of sympathy, the dawdled retreat and resumption of talk speculative and curious in which everyone shared.

'I was paying, so I didn't see,' Earl told her. 'Len did, though. He pushed me back and vaulted over the counter as if it were a five-bar gate. Incredible. Wonder if anyone from Granada spotted it.'

She tried to smile but her lips described the imminence of tears.

'I heard what he said, though. I'm sorry. You got what should have come to me.'

She shook her head.

'Yes. It's happened before. Some men are quite sincerely revolted; they say it's not natural, rationalizing a kind of primeval fear. Which is a laugh, isn't it? When they are just sufficiently inhibited not to insult me, they spit their venom over the girl.'

'He wanted to know what you did.'

'Exactly. A pity you didn't have time to explain.' His grin cajoled but she could not respond. 'I haven't heard it put quite like that before, but it's the usual assumption – that blacks are permanently and gigantically tumescent.'

'I wouldn't know about that,' trying to giggle.

'That's better.' He put his arms round her. 'Sorry I can't oblige.'

'That's twice you've apologized for nothing.'

'I meant it both times, Olivia. You're the nearest any woman has come to causing me regret.'

'Regret! Don't say that, Earl. Not tonight.'

For tonight it was harder to be forsaken. She needed his warmth, his body tucked round hers, shutting out the sight of the man's face. And as he kissed her cheek, there in view of Len and the rest of his customers, the tears finally gushed. Because she was the wrong sex.

Chapter Four

It had been ridiculous to behave like that, Olivia repri-
manded herself over breakfast. Her feelings for Earl had
stabilized months before when she had finally accepted
his preference. Silently, because she did not wish him
to suspect a hope that he had never encouraged. So an
infatuation that might have developed into an emotion
more solid had passed into a friendship generous and
almost as affectionate as any she had. However, it
seemed that the pangs of love had not been entirely
quietened, she acknowledged satirically; they could
produce the occasional twitch. For the previous evening
she would have staked everything – their unspoken
agreement and friendship – to have brought him to her
bed. Which astonished her. She had no desire for intimacy with Earl.

'Even were that offered, I wouldn't want it,' she had
once confessed to Judy. 'Kissing, the usual touching, is
fine, but merely the thought of anything more fills me
with disgust. It's the idea of men with him that bugs me.
I'm as bad as the population at large.'

Judy had laughed. 'In this instance I'd stay with them
since an attempt at seduction would definitely be a
waste of time! You're disappointed, that's all; a touch
of sour grapes. I imagine you'd be just as much bugged
by the idea of a woman with him.'

But Olivia had not agreed.

Ten hours earlier she had not felt squeamish; she had
wanted him to help her through the night. It was a
simple need, the urgency to repair self-valuation splin-

tered by the man's words, to prove that despite them she was desirable. Again she was astonished. She had been harassed before, and though never so viciously or in such terms, she was dismayed by this episode's effect. It was like a physical assault, and Earl's explanation had heightened not soothed the bruise.

She was disappointed in herself. Her reaction to the man had been his success; his power had been endorsed by the sight of her fear. But, shocked, she had been unable to summon a detachment. As she looked back, the whole evening had the tempo of a cardiograph's needle describing a feverish pulse. She must cure this; there was the audition on Saturday. For which she must rehearse her pieces, be calm and relaxed.

Olivia finished her breakfast, stacked the crockery on a tray by the electric fire, collected towel and clothes. She knew that the most valuable preparation for Saturday would be to find Rita Dale.

On the landing Mrs Winterton met her with: 'I think I should mention, Olivia, that our telephone is very popular suddenly, even allowing for agency business. Someone called three times while you were out yesterday evening.'

'The same person?'

'I was given no opportunity to inquire since the caller put down the telephone as soon as I answered it. I'd be grateful, my dear, if you would issue a gentle rebuke. I don't know what is the current practice but I consider it discourteous to ring off without an apology for bringing the wrong person to the phone. I'm always ready to take a message.'

She was certainly the wrong person, Olivia thought. 'I'm sorry. I don't know him.'

'A prospective young swain or an unidentified bad lot?'

'If the former, he's so smitten he's tongue-tied. I had hoped that you wouldn't be bothered.'

'Since I live here, that was not very likely. If I'm right in deducing that you wished to protect an old woman from unnecessary annoyance,' she deduced correctly, 'then I'm touched but a little irritated. I am not yet senile. I can still contemplate, though with repugnance, the affairs of this world. When did these nuisance calls begin?'

Chastened, Olivia explained.

'I'd say that on the first occasion the choice of number was totally random,' Mrs Winterton reasoned, 'but after that it was remembered and became automatic. To imagine that the selection was deliberate is somewhat extravagant. Though admittedly the improbable is not impossible. Ten years on the Bench taught me that no abnormalities are . . . impossible. But I cannot understand why you should think this is directed only at you.'

'I have the feeling it is.'

The other tutted. 'You have too much free time, which encourages brooding, Olivia. It will be a good day for more than your pocket when you get work.'

She smiled agreement. Faced with the woman's robust sense, her conviction was irrational, an egocentric indulgence. Perhaps, after so long without applause, she wanted attention.

'Few people can know this is your number,' Mrs Winterton pointed out. 'Neither is your name in the directory.'

Through the open door of the bathroom and beyond its window marbled by rain and grime Olivia could see sheds, plank gates crooked between high brick walls, the pewter-grey dust of an alley; then mirroring this, the back of the next street whose windows looked across, their stealthy regard lidded in net. Which hers, this bathroom neglected but for her use, did not have. Unfrosted, the glass reminded her of the discrepant panes in the front door and her stomach was twisted again by the threat of the telephone's silence within the colluding moon. 'If he knew I lived here – knew which house – how could he get the telephone number?'

Impatient, Mrs Winterton leant forward and slapped her wrist. 'Drat you, girl, for being so foolish. I'm certain the calls are merely chance. Why should anyone wish to upset you? You've done nothing to provoke such nastiness. And though I have quite a reputation in these parts and from time to time excite a good deal of antagonism, unbridled criticism of the management of the Old People's Home scarcely merits systematic and anonymous vexation.'

If she's so well known, Olivia thought, plenty of people could tell him who lives here, then he only had to look up the name in the directory. He would know that the younger voice was hers. Or he might work for Telecom.

'No doubt the caller will grow bored shortly or find some more satisfactory way of occupying his – or her – time,' the other went on; 'but if the tiresome business continues I shall ask the exchange to intercept incoming calls. The disadvantage about that is its effect on the innocent. Asked to state the number she required, my sister Dorothy would be struck with incurable amnesia. However, that is a risk I may have to take. Should we receive any more of these calls today, I will attend to them before I leave – late this afternoon. I'm going to visit my nephew and shall insist that he take his wife out while I look after the children. I shall pack a nightgown to prevent argument. I enjoy a treat occasionally,' referring to a weekly habit. 'The dust can wait until I get back.'

It was very patient, Olivia thought, smiling; it had hung about so long that it had probably forgotten, along with Mrs Winterton, what it was waiting for.

There was no dust in the front room of the house in Cattlegate and the soot had been washed from the hearth; but unrefreshed by a breeze from an open window and not rumpled by the movements of living warmth, the air lay musty and flat.

This was acknowledged by the woman who invited her in. 'We come in the back as a rule,' she said, bolting the door and replacing its chain. 'Charlotte likes this kept tidy. She's out at the minute, roaming, and he's at work, so there'll not be repercussions if we go into the kitchen. The kettle's on low, ready, always is, but if you'd like a cup of tea I can soon put it on again, after. I'm Dora Booth, her mother.'

Charlotte's devotion to polish was more reticent in the kitchen. Concessions had been made, presumably reluctant, to its use, and though very clean it bore signs of occupation: knitting poked from under a cushion; the toes of shoes peeped from beneath the sideboard; ironed clothes reached down from the rack above the hearth; a line of unripe tomatoes knobbed the window-sill, beckoning the sun.

'I see you've got our Rita's umbrella,' the woman said from the scullery.

'Yes. I've brought it back. That's why I've come.'

'Well, we don't see much of her nowadays but I'll keep it till she's next round, or leave it out for her. She's got a key so she can always get in. Are you a friend of hers, then?'

Unprepared for a woman who appeared not to know that her granddaughter was missing, Olivia floundered. 'Sort of.'

'Sort of? Doesn't sound like much of a friend to me.' Water swilled in the sink then she was at the door, nursing the teapot. 'But our Rita's never do. Never seem to stick, except now and again. I tell her you can't expect the earth, only I do reckon she would have done better than those she's had.'

'But I'm not one of them,' Olivia defended. 'I'm just returning this.'

'At least you're honest. I must say not many would bother. It's like Rita to lend out to strangers.' She scooped tea from the caddy and went back to the kettle.

'She didn't. Mr Dale lent me the umbrella on Monday.' It was a small point to struggle over but she wanted to clear it up.

'That's right,' Mrs Booth answered serenely. 'Now I think on, they mentioned you'd been.'

'And I've never met Rita,' she persisted.

'Haven't you now? In that case, I've been speaking out of turn.' With a swift change of tone, the woman discarded accusation. 'Between ourselves, you haven't missed a lot, not if you like company. I'll not have persons say anything against Rita, she's my flesh and blood, but it's my opinion she hasn't got the way with folks you need. Not like her mother's uncle Charles. That's why I called her Charlotte, you see, hoping that a bit would rub off. Life and soul of the party, he is. People loved him as a lad; give him their last shilling if he asked. I've brewed it strong so it'll take more water after the first couple of cups,' carrying these and saucers to the table.

'Are you saying that Rita is shy?' She must make herself ask questions even if they did not seem pertinent to her search.

'She's not so much shy as not easy, on the awkward side, won't let herself go. Don't tell me you're another young 'un that refuses sugar; to my mind tea's like slops without. Have a biscuit; there's nothing like a spot of tea and biscuit of a morning if you're allowed.'

Permission granted by Charlotte's absence, they both selected a biscuit from the tin. Mrs Booth sighed contentedly. 'Nice of you to call round. Are you visiting?' She's already forgotten, Olivia thought, but before she could, mistakenly, remind her, the other added, 'I can see you're not from these parts.'

'How?'

55

'By the way you talk. But I've nothing against it within reason. Not like some. I'm ready to keep an open mind even if a body does talk posh.'

Not discomforted by this candour since in a comparable situation she could have employed it herself, though without the regional conceit, Olivia answered, 'I'm not necessarily a visitor because I talk like this. Most people that I've met round here do.'

'Funny I don't meet them; but then, it's bingo for me, not bridge.' Her look was hostile, placing Olivia amongst those who occasioned her resentful contempt.

Again there had been no warning for this abrupt shift of tone and, annoyed at being for a second time unjustly accused but anxious to restore their former amity, Olivia resorted to a spontaneous performance. She took a gulp of her tea, wiped her mouth with the back of her hand as if rehearsed by Alan, and pronounced in an accent woven from mill smoke, fell mists and dyed-in-the-wool yarns: 'As I say t'wife, for them after nowt butta comfortable flutter, bingo's handy.'

There was a moment's quiet, that dreadful hiatus for the decision between bouquets and rotten eggs, then Mrs Booth's cup clattered in its saucer as she rocked back and the room took the blast of her trumpeting whoops.

'You're a rare one,' she said at last. 'Just look what you've made me do,' and after a number of false starts tipped the tea in her saucer back into the cup. 'You're as bad as my brother Charlie; he's a card, he is, and never better than when taking folks off. Should've been on the halls, but they were before his time. You ever thought of anything like that?'

'I'm an actress.'

'Get away with you! You're having me on.'

'No; I'm not.' Encouraged, Olivia talked about her profession and, because she assumed that Mrs Booth wanted only the excitements of grease-paint and lights,

56

the thrill of an expectant audience and the noise of applause, she censored the rest: the apprehension, the fatigue, the present emptiness, so that for a brief space those did not exist. Sitting stage centre, surrounded by meticulously chosen props, placed before the window's cyclorama and with a rack of clothes forming the tabs above her head, she enjoyed a solace in the deceit. But it was short-lived.

The other questioned, 'Did you act in that film they made about Rita?'

So she did know that Rita was missing but had not admitted it, taking the umbrella with no word or sign of distress. Her description of the girl had been unsentimental, not falsified by an anticipated grief. She was confident that Rita would be found and though this optimism was matched to Olivia's need, she found it disturbing; it was complacent and facile. Convinced that Rita would reappear in the future, Mrs Booth accepted her unexplained absence without curiosity or alarm.

'Well,' she prompted, 'did you take any part in it?'

'Yes; I did,' and Olivia heard herself stuttering because by 'part' the other did not mean a theatrical role; she charged complicity. 'I was Elizabeth Drew.'

'Her Rita lives with? Waste of time, I'd say.'

'It was a job; the first that's come up for months.'

'And we've all got to eat,' the woman conceded. 'I can see it's not all roses, being an actress, if it's like that. But they had no business putting it on telly, poking their noses in. I wouldn't watch it, but Charlotte and him did, and they told me.'

'It might help to find her.'

'Not if she doesn't want. She's biding her time, takes after Charlie in that. Until she's ready wild horses won't drag her out.'

Olivia took another mouthful of tea; lukewarm, it was blamed for the nausea in her throat.

'Won't drag her out of where, Mrs Booth?' She had to humour her.

'Out of where she's hid. She's stubborn, is Rita. You wouldn't have said so when she was little, always did as she was told, but that's how she's gone: stubborn. Look how she left here. Not long finished schooling, and she's up off. Her father would have kept her, he's not a bad one in that respect, he'd have seen she wasn't short. But no, would she be doing with that? Not Rita. She's got the supplementary benefit, she says, so she can do by herself. Living in the same town, with a proper home here for her! Charlotte'll never live down the disgrace.'

'It's natural to want to be independent.' But she was beginning to like Rita.

'Ay, and it seems it's natural to ride roughshod over them that are older, with not so much as a sorry when you've hurt. But young 'uns are always the same.' She paused, rubbing an arthritic knuckle, then more calmly, 'I can't pretend I was any different. I was the second in a row of nine and my mother always promised herself a rest when I'd left school and could help out. But I didn't think much of that and was soon looking round. Married my Bob no more than three months after he'd popped the question and had four of my own inside five years. Talk about out of the frying pan!' She cackled harshly. 'Served me right. You'll have another cup? Topping up'll not drown the pot.'

'Thank you.' Waiting, Olivia considered how to return the conversation to Rita while avoiding reference to her disappearance. She did not wish to hear again the assertion that the girl was biding her time. It was a piece of lunacy glinting from the bedrock of practical sense.

'I expect your mother got used to your leaving home,' she said as casually as she could manage, stirring her tea. 'Just as mine has,' and did not blink at the lie. 'And eventually Mrs Dale won't mind as much, will she? If

Rita is anything like I was a few years ago, I reckon there'll be a lot of compensations.'

Mrs Booth laughed. 'A bit of a harum-scarum, were you? I'd not be surprised. But Rita wasn't, not till this blew up, and I'd be telling a lie if I said I didn't sometimes feel like giving her a push; she was altogether too quiet, seemed to lack spirit, but it seems I was wrong. She had spirit enough when she'd made up her mind. Or perhaps it was a case of the worm turning. It was the way she did it that wasn't right, in my view. Got all her bags packed and stacked on the pavement, then comes into this kitchen and announces she's off. And she didn't mince her words, either. They didn't bother me. I know when I'm right; but Charlotte is a different matter and was cut deep. It was a long time, too, before they found out where she was. Rita has a crafty streak and she kept herself close, but Charlotte was always out looking and one night when she saw her leaving a pub she followed her and got the address. She didn't visit but she was able to keep tabs on her. That settled her down a bit.'

Though she sat in the path of the tunnelling sun, Olivia shivered. A woman thrown off by her child was a desolate figure, but she was a wretch possessed as she travelled the streets. Which she was doing once more: roaming, as Mrs Booth had said, her steps paced by the hope of a chance sight. Because she had found her daughter on that other occasion and would do so again. The belief was irrational and its intensity terrible, leaving the woman no resource against disproof. Frightened, Olivia was suddenly gripped by doubt.

'Until this last lot, that is,' Mrs Booth continued. 'She'd have been better off not knowing about it, in my opinion. Rita'll turn up again when it suits. But some busybody next door saw the milk and went along to the police station, so a constable came round. How they got this address, I'll never know; you can't keep anything to yourself nowadays, but round he came and before long Charlotte was in a state again, what with having to say that Rita had left home and the questions. I went after him when he was going and told him not to put himself out; it's a family matter. He said it was only a routine visit and he wouldn't be taking it any further unless something suspicious turned up. He wasn't there to get persons who'd flitted because they couldn't pay the rent or such. Will you have another biscuit?

'Of course I didn't know whether he meant our Rita or the other one, but that didn't bother me; and I reckoned him saying that settled the business and I told Charlotte as much; but then the telly got on to it – tongues must wag sixty to the dozen in that street – and they must have got licence to go into the house. Charlotte didn't like that but she gave them a photo, they were that pressing and telling her all the time they'd find Rita for her. Left her room in a state by all accounts, too, cheeky buggers.'

'That's how they found it.'

'So they say but I wouldn't put it past them to mucky it up if they were after a show.' Her description fell short of vandalism but Olivia did not correct it; there was enough general truth in Mrs Booth's prejudice to discourage argument. 'Do anything, some folks will, to get others hotted up. Take that reporter. If I'd had my way I'd have shown him the door and as things turned out I'd have been right.'

'I didn't know that the press had got on to it.'

'Only the *Evening Chronicle*; the *Post* wouldn't condescend. We're not important enough for them,' indicating an ambivalent attitude to publicity. 'The young man was nice enough, seemingly, but he got round Charlotte with his sighing and clucking and put ideas in her head which would have been best left out. She was upset as it was, being told Rita had gone again after months spent looking, but she was in a real state by the time he'd left.

Doing a follow-up, as he called it, of the telly, asking questions, only not like the constable. All he wanted to know was things like dates, when she left and the last time we'd seen her. This newspaper man wasn't satisfied with that. No; he wanted what he called the story. I told him there wasn't one but he took no notice of that and claimed the state of Rita's room looked fishy. "I've known tidier than our Rita," I told him but that didn't stop him.'

'Was he suggesting that she had been attacked or something?'

'He wouldn't go as far as that but he did say that some person must have it in for her. "You should've seen her bedroom here," I told him and he gave me a look like I was three sheets to the wind. "It's you that's barmy," I said. "Our Rita's not the sort to provoke such nastiness." '

It was strange to hear this echo of Mrs Winterton but not really surprising, Olivia thought; the argument was obvious. Unfortunately, nastiness often had no excuse for being provoked. She thought of Alan. It was true that she had risen to his sarcasm over her friendship with Judy, but surely that should not have incited him to speak so maliciously.

'So he went off that and asked about her landlady,' Mrs Booth was saying. 'You know her, that Mrs Drew.'

'No, I don't know her. I represented her.'

'Of course. I was forgetting. Charlotte said you looked very like.'

'I didn't know she'd met her.'

'She was going on the telly.'

About to inquire when Mrs Drew had appeared on television, Olivia realized the muddle. Incredulity gagged an attempt to clear it up.

'Charlotte hadn't anything against her, that is to say, personally, not till that chap from the *Evening Chronicle* came round. He was a sly one, asking questions in a way

61

that put words in her mouth. As I said to Charlotte, no landlady throws a lodger's things about, she wants the place kept respectable, even if there is something going on.'

'What sort of thing?'

'You might well ask, my dear, and he wouldn't come straight out with it. Mentioned a journalist's instinct, something to do with his nose, though I wouldn't have drawn attention to that if I'd been him, never seen such a conk on a man, took him round in circles and us with him, too, asking what footing they were on and whether we were happy with Rita living with that type. I asked him what he meant by that and I must say he had the grace to blush. "I'm afraid I'm not at liberty to answer that," he says, "but I appreciate how a mother must feel when her daughter gets a pull to leave a nice home like this." Smarmy young know-all.'

'Mrs Drew has gone away as well.'

'That's what he said. "And what's so funny about that?" I asked him. "We've come to a pretty pass if you have to stick up a notice every time you leave the house." That's what two wars have done for us – identity cards, numbers by your name, reporting to them behind desks if you've earned a few extra bob to give a bit of spice to your pension. Might as well be locked up, I sometimes think, for all the difference it makes. But there's some that give it the slip.' She paused. Slowly, her voice low but vibrant, she continued, 'Ay, there's some that'll not have tabs kept on them. They're the lucky ones. They were blessed with the fairy touch.' Again she paused and, smiling, her face changed; its severity was smoothed into gentleness; its lines recalled dimples and the look she gave Olivia was a girl's, winsome, carefree, lit by the unbarred sun.

'Here,' she said, rising, and tapped her guest's arm. 'I'll show you.'

Opening a door in the corner of the kitchen, she led

Olivia up a funnel of narrow stairs lit by a skylight above. At their head was the bedroom looking on to the street, and four steps along a passage barely a man's width was a door to the room over the kitchen. 'Rita's,' her guide said as they passed. The third bedroom, above the scullery which projected from the main structure into the yard, would be smaller, Olivia knew, and in such terraces these were sometimes converted into bathrooms with the help of council grants. They rarely offered enough space for a full-size bed. Neither did the one she was looking in now, but it was impossible to determine whether its dimensions were at fault; the immediate reason was what it contained.

'Go on in.' The woman drew Olivia past her and into the tiny well at the centre. 'I keep it dusted. You have a good look,' she urged from the door.

Unwillingly, feeling like a trespasser, Olivia let her eyes skim round the room, over tables, chests, shelves, cabinets, anything that offered a surface for hoarded possessions, faded, yellowing, threadbare, warped and curled by years of the changing seasons and the fingering light but laid out with affection, brushed or cleaned with vigilant love. Her glance arrested by a pair of knitted bootees felted by washing but threaded with new ribbon and placed in a nest of lace, Olivia began to examine as the other wished and saw the wooden rattle impressed by small teeth, the hoop, the stringed whip and the top chevroned with coloured chalks, the birds' eggs neatly blown, a bicycle clip, a pile of cigarette cards, then the cigarette packets themselves, Gold Flake still lustrous but empty, a football, a collar stud, a cigarette lighter, its brass buffed to gold, then letters, magazines, a time sheet, the progressing memorabilia of a man.

'There's more in that trunk,' Mrs Booth told her; 'things that 'ud soon spoil if left out, like what he was christened in. And I keep his watch safe in a box, it was his granddad's, he wouldn't take that with him. Solid gold it is, and he wears it as meant with the chain across his chest when he gets himself up. I haven't let anything go.' She waved round the room. 'Though there's some that wouldn't think twice about getting rid of it, given half the chance, but Charlotte always backs me up. Takes a good picture, doesn't he? I've got an album full in that drawer and I change them over the end of every month so they all get an airing.'

Nodded towards a cabinet, Olivia looked at the photographs. Not knowing which face she should praise, she skirted a group of footballers and peered at a young man astride a motor bike, grinning, slightly impertinent. He reminded her of someone she thought she should know.

'That bike wasn't his,' the other interpreted. 'He'd borrowed it for a lark. Allus doing something to give you a laugh.'

By the side of this there was another in an ornate silver frame; it showed him dressed as a soldier, a man little older than herself, laughing across the years.

A third photograph of him was on the sideboard in Charlotte Dale's front room.

'Is he your son?'

'Mine were all girls, more's the pity. That's Charlie. Of course, there's a lot here'll be no use to him: he's a bit big for rompers!' she chuckled, happy. 'But there's his civvies in the trunk; I wash them every Whitsun so they stay fresh, and when she was a little one Rita would clean his boots but she got so's she wouldn't, I'll never know why. There's not another that could have a great-uncle like him.'

Great-uncle. Olivia leant against the table trying to calculate, but she knew that was not necessary.

'When do you expect him back?' she asked, forcing her voice to remain even.

'Any time. I can wait. I've been waiting this last forty year or more. I've the patience; he'll not catch me out.

The kettle's always on the hob and his best togs ready. You like what I've done, then?'

Her stomach lurching, Olivia nodded obediently but could not look into the woman's eyes. They were blind to the knowledge that she had brought Olivia to a private shrine.

' "Don't you be worriting, Dora," he said on his last leave. "I'll be out of this lot sooner than you think." He wasn't cut out for the Army, didn't like being at anybody's beck and call, so I knew what he meant. When he was reported missing I didn't take any notice. Missing, was the way They put it, believed dead. Well, Charlie wasn't made to stop bullets. No; he'd taken a chance when he saw it coming, but then, you see, he had to lie low. Stick him in prison if they found him and that wouldn't suit. Always as free as the wind is Charlie. As I said, it's granted to some and he's one of the lucky ones. He'll not be cooped up. Not like Charlotte or me.'

Chapter Five

Reaching a low wall by the side of the supermarket, Olivia sat down to recover her breath. For a second time she had fled from the Dales' house; for a second time they had offered her an experience with which she could not cope. She was appalled by her inadequacy. She was nearly twenty-one; her life had not been particularly sheltered; she had come across eccentricities, neuroses, the disintegration in the clamp of failure or loss, but she had never met anything like this: a woman sensible, astringent, vigorous yet animated by an insane belief. Perhaps this wasn't so abnormal; perhaps lots of people had this in some degree which accounted for extravagant conduct. Such as Alan and the man the previous night. But this must be different. A forty-year vigil! She wondered how it had started. From the error that 'Missing, believed dead' concealed a hope? From the adoration of a sister that refused to be bereaved?

She flattered herself that she had perception and sympathies but Mrs Booth had defeated her. Brushed by the relics of a man long dead, she could not talk of his homecoming; only condolences would wrinkle her lips. So she had stood silent, wishing she could stop her ears to the woman's plans: banners across the street which had welcomed back others, the outings, the parties in honour of a hero returning, handsome, rollicking, ungrizzled by time. Until finally she had escaped on the back of excuses which had been accepted as truth but were an expression of cowardice.

She must buy food, go home and make a sandwich. That might calm her stomach. She felt sick. No wonder that Rita had left home. She was seventeen. Seventeen years of that! Acquiescent when she was a child, cleaning his boots, but as she grew older less patiently deferring to the intrusion of a woman who waited on a ghost.

'There isn't much room left for you,' Olivia had said, trying to restore the commonplace.

'I don't need any more. His are enough for me. I wouldn't mind sleeping on the sofa in the kitchen but Charlotte won't have that so I climb in with Rita.' In order that his cenotaph should remain undisturbed.

Mrs Booth had said earlier, 'She didn't mince her words but that didn't bother me. I know when I'm right.' Presumably Rita had at last had the courage to denounce her grandmother's obsession. Which her mother may share, for Rita's words had 'cut her deep'.

This must explain Mr Dale's ghastly insistence that his wife 'prepare herself for the worst'. He knew what the opposite 'can lead to'. He spoke out of the haunting of years as he sat in a room whose funereal atmosphere was appropriate to his choice. While upstairs in that divided house was a woman devoted to an impossible resurrection. Olivia did not know which scared her the more.

But Rita's mother refused to be coerced by her husband. She was out, roaming; Rita had been found once and would be again. And now Olivia was grateful for this persistence; it affirmed life, though she was revolted by the suspicion that Mrs Dale was influenced by her mother's faith in another's return.

She had nothing to prove that, however, only hints that Mrs Dale was sympathetic towards her mother's delusions. Earl had warned her against theories that were far-fetched. Olivia got up from the wall and strode into the supermarket, thinking: the reasons why Mrs Dale continues her search are irrelevant; what matters is that she is doing it. She hoped that the woman was making more progress than she. All she had come across so far was a friend called Karen who didn't even know that Rita was missing, Stephen who said that she never stayed long in one place, and a soldier's monument.

She had learnt something about Rita, though, but she must be careful about that, she warned herself as she picked up a basket. If she began to create a character, discover the feelings, the attitudes, the motives behind the behaviour, she would become immersed in it and that would be dangerous. Rita wasn't a girl in a play, a fictitious person bodied out for the length of the performance, given a truth dependent on art, wholly absorbing and alive for a small space, then shed. Rita existed. She wasn't born in the imagination of a dramatist then realized by the skill of an actress. She wasn't confined to a three-hour show; she belonged to the same cycle of hours as did Olivia and their re-creation might take over Olivia's own. Fearing this, she told herself that she must concentrate upon the situation. To find that, to discover what had happened and trace the girl was more scientific; it was a job she had undertaken and it would be conducted more successfully if she were detached. But she knew that was already denied her because from the moment she had opened the door of Elizabeth Drew's house and had run down the path, she had felt involved. It had begun then, as she had tried to tell Earl. Perhaps it was the house, she argued to herself, so similar to Mrs Winterton's though she had seen only the hall, and Alan hanging about waiting for his cue, stopping her before the take of her scene to ask when was Judy's next visit. It was as if that morning's work had been a piece of make-believe, as if it were not a film she was taking part in but a segment of her own life that she was hurrying through. And though it should have been humdrum and unmemorable, it carried a hint of crisis, a warning that something of value was at risk and the swift pinch of personal danger. Did it seem like that at the time? she asked herself. Or has the occasion sprouted all that in the memory, a poisonous fungus whose spores are a kerb crawler and a phone's silent threat?

There was no sense in dwelling on those; she must apply herself to her task. Over lunch she would be systematic; she would try to recall all the comments of people she had met and see if they were related. As, thinking of this, she regarded a row of tins without seeing the labels, Olivia felt the tug of an examining stare.

'I thought you were someone else for a minute, but you're not a bit like her, when you look close,' the woman stammered. 'Sorry,' and moved away.

'That's all right. Do you mean Elizabeth Drew?'

The other stopped. 'Yes. It was just that I haven't got my glasses; they got broke. I should've known first off it wasn't Elizabeth. She wouldn't let me pass without a word.'

'How long is it since you've seen her?'

'I don't know.' She expressed no surprise at the question, just as it appeared quite natural that Olivia also knew the woman. 'It could be three weeks or more. It's not easy to get round.'

'Do you know she's not living in her house at the moment?'

'A neighbour over the way told me it was in Monday's paper, on account of the young girl: I can't remember her name.'

A small child wedged in the trolley's stocks began to whine; fatigue dragged at the woman's face.

'Rita Dale. I suppose the two of them disappearing near the same time must be simply a coincidence?'

The woman took a dummy out of her pocket, wiped it on her sleeve, sucked it and pushed it into the child's mouth. 'Coincidence?' she repeated. The word was effortful, too long; it measured the distance between them. 'I wouldn't know about that. Maybe it was best getting out of the way for a bit.'

'Out of the way of what?' She was conscious of the interrogation, that she was subordinating the woman with the authority of health, articulateness and freedom from ties.

'Everything. She always says she's lucky. She can clear out, but when ructions come I haven't the chance.'

'I don't understand what you're talking about.'

The other looked at her. 'No, I can see that,' she answered with a flick of bitterness. Then, 'Let's hope you never do.'

When you reach a dead-end, Olivia advised herself, just turn back and try another route. 'Have you any idea where Rita Dale might have gone?'

'Why should I have? I expect there was a reason. We never talked but I knew she was there.' The hands on the trolley began to shake. 'If you're from the police then I'm telling you I know nothing about it.'

'I'm not from the police.'

'That's just as well. If I was seen talking to one of them, it 'ud be taken wrong. I'll have to go. I've been longer than I ought and it'll be noticed. There's the baby outside in the pram and she'll need feeding.'

Clumsily she slid the trolley into a tight arc and followed it towards the till, her back humped inside the shiny pilled cardigan, her scraggy thighs silhouetted under the flimsy transparent skirt, the sandals broken and white legs prematurely veined. Watching her, Olivia saw that the neglect was not only that of poverty but of defeat; and thought, could I ever become like that?

She stood by the shelves of tinned meat and looked about her, considering for the first time the nature of what she saw. Since coming to the town she had shopped there weekly, using the place as a quick convenience. Absorbed in her own affairs, a transient, someone who did not belong to the town, she had hurried through purchases and had left with no more acute sensation than one of distaste. Now she gave the shop her attention. It hardly qualified as a supermarket; the name was a hopeful make-believe for three corridors of shelves on which were stacked tins, dried milk and sliced bread. At one end a concession had been made to less restricted diets by a rack of bruised onions, a few rotting carrots and wizened potatoes sustaining pallid shoots. At the other end a more realistic understanding of customers' requirements was indicated in a heap of sanitary towels, a card of children's dummies almost empty, tablets of aspirin and, by the till, packets of cigarettes. Even had the dust been removed from the tins, the place would have been irrevocably squalid: a packet of biscuits, staved in, leaked a gritty scurf; a dispenser of strawberry sauce, experimentally squeezed, still oozed red; bags of sugar, their stay too brief to justify shelving, remained in cartons on the floor; and rashed densely over the curling linoleum tiles were the jet scabs of discarded chewing gum, tufted with hairs or sticky with spills. And Olivia thought, did Rita come here? Did Rita, after leaving the neat cleanliness of her home, having to live as I do on the dole, come here and feel smirched by its ugliness, be revolted by the dirt and depressed by the apathy which make it such a horrible place? Perhaps she had come but, like Olivia, had not noticed; or had resembled the shuffling customers who seemed not to care. Or more likely, reared in the town she had simply received this as a natural feature. She would be no objective observer. Yet Olivia was taken with an irrational impulse to protect and, striding to the till, asked, 'Does Rita Dale shop here?'

The man put his finger under a sentence in the magazine, looked up and considered while she willed a negative.

'Was she the one on the telly?'

'Yes.'

'I thought I recognized you.

'I'm asking about the other one, the girl in the photograph.'

'That wasn't much use, was it? Must have been taken years ago, working it out from what they said in the paper. But I knew it was you the moment you came in. Have they found her yet? They was hoping you'd come forward.'

This time she did not pause. 'I'm not the woman she lodged with. I just pretended to be her.'

'Funny sort of job, going round taking off someone else. Wouldn't do for me. I'd soon get myself in a pickle. Still, there might be something in it,' he reflected, 'if it's bigamy you're interested in.'

'I'm not.'

'Takes all sorts. You want this checked out?'

Olivia wondered what else he imagined she might want done with the goods, but nodded.

'Not as much as usual,' he commented.

'I don't generally buy any more.'

'See what I mean? Like I said, if you set out to be two folks, you can get so you don't know t'other from which. You lose track. Mostly it's ten or fifteen quid.'

'Not for me,' she insisted. 'You must be thinking of the other one.'

She immediately regretted the correction. He glared resentfully. 'I'm not thinking of any on yer,' he snapped, punching the keys of his machine. 'I'm here to take the cash, not waste time admiring the mugs of customers. So don't blame me if a couple on you look the same. And if one has the habit of putting me to the trouble of ringing up no more than a miserly three pounds seventy, then don't be surprised if I don't recall it chapter and verse. The other one, or you, depending on which way the wind's blowing, was a proper customer. They can say what they like, that's nowt to do with me, because she paid on the nail and never let out a word of com-

72

plaint, though now and again they'd forgot to deliver the new bread. "You feed them too well," I used to tell her, though it wasn't in my interests. "How many you got?" "Just the one," she'd say, "but still growing. At least, that's the excuse." '

So, whatever was implied by the reference to gossip, Elizabeth Drew had been a satisfactory customer and had not stinted Rita. The arrangement between them clearly went further than letting a room. Remembering the photograph's pathetic defensiveness, Olivia reflected that the other woman must have responded to a need. And though she had not eaten that day, or probably because of that since hunger induced a kind of somnolence, Olivia turned from the direction of her lodgings and walked though the unfamiliar streets towards the house of Elizabeth Drew.

It was not until she had reached it, private again after the inquisitive cameras, that she wondered why she had come and, feeling suddenly shy and discomforted by this involuntary inspection, she excused her hesitation at the gate by closing it gently, then turned to go. A tap on a window prevented her. Looking up, she saw a woman in the adjacent house beckon.

'I thought it was her for a minute,' the neighbour greeted her from the door, 'but then I saw it was you. When my hubby was watching that programme he said, "You've done a nice job there, Laura." It was my description, you see, that the television went for and when they brought round your photo I said, "That's the one. To a T." '

'Thank you,' Olivia said since that seemed expected. Also, the woman was responsible for providing her with half a day's work.

The neighbour preened herself. 'I didn't mind being put out a bit. Do you get called upon much?'

'Not as a double. That sort of work's limited, I hope.'

Unsmiling, the other nodded. 'You could say it's a

waste of time and money if nothing comes of it. It hasn't fetched her back, or found little Rita.' She lowered herself down the steps then bustled the four paces to the gate. 'It's her we have to worry ourselves about. The moment she came, I said to my hubby, "Next door's no place for a young girl." '

'Why was that?'

The woman glanced up the street and checked for eavesdroppers. Seeing none but a mangy dog methodically refreshing his territory, she leant over the gate and whispered, 'Men.'

It was clear that some horrified answer was required. Unable to comply, Olivia merely contrived to look startled and stammered, 'Did Rita have a lot of boyfriends, then?'

The other shook her head impatiently. 'Not Rita! *Her!*'

'Really?'

'Round knocking every verse end. In the middle of the night mostly, and drunk as lords. Disgusting. Woke all the street. Funny-looking oddities, too, for the most part. They hadn't seen water for weeks. As Frank said, the nearest they'd ever got to water was beer. He's a comic at times, is Frank.

'I went out when it first started to ask them to show a bit of consideration for others but they didn't take any notice and Frank said better keep out of it else they'd start knocking here, so I took to banging on the wall.'

Reluctantly suppressing the obvious comment, Olivia nodded.

'Got a reputation for herself up the street, one way or another,' and before Olivia could frame a request for definition of the various ways, she went on, 'but nobody interfered, of course; there was no proof. Rita wasn't the only one either, you know. I could have put their minds at rest about that, but naturally I didn't go round telling tales.'

I bet you didn't, Olivia commented silently. 'Wasn't she?'

'Not a bit of it.'

It wasn't that her talent for interrogation was improving, Olivia told herself, but that there was an understood convention: prompts were required not to encourage the speaker but to maintain the suspense and give a semblance of dialogue.

'There were others coming at all hours. "I can't understand what any decent young man can see in half of them," I said to Frank and he pointed out the callers were hardly decent so perhaps they weren't so choosy; none of them in the house were what you might call oil paintings.'

'Weren't they?'

'Except *her*,' she added hurriedly but conceded only that Elizabeth Drew would pass in a crowd. 'You flatter her. When the television brought the photo I told them, "She's like, but the drawback is, she's better favoured." '

Irritated but controlling her tone, Olivia remarked, 'It will be interesting to compare, if we ever meet.'

'Well, you live here, don't you? One from the telly said. So you might; she's never away for long. Except that I wouldn't be surprised if after this little lot we hadn't seen the last of her. I saw her going off, you know, cool as a cucumber, as well as that lad from the telephone exchange, but they would choose to put him in the picture. After all I'd done! I thought it best to report it, after hearing that car one morning – only it shot off before I could get to the window; but as my hubby says, I can't be expected to be responsible for the whole street – and then what with her going and the milk piling up on the step, it looked suspicious to me. As I said to Mr Garbutt, "That Mrs Drew must have left little Rita there by herself for a bit because she'd have been sure to remember to cancel the milk if the house was going to be empty, whereas a young one is more feckless." Only it wasn't my business to stop other folk's milk – I'd not get any thanks for that – so I went to the police.

'They came round grumbling and fetched in Mr Catchpole who lets this row but they all slipped in and out without as much as a word in my direction. First thing I knew about the way Rita's bedroom had been smashed up was watching the telly. "Well, did you ever?" I said to Mr Garbutt. "They can come here asking me to judge photographs but they don't think that puts them under any obligation to give a hint of what it's for." "You'll know what to do next time, Laura," he says; "you'll keep quiet and let them shift for themselves. See what a job they can make of that." And then when Monday night's paper came out and it said that about violence, I said to him, "They should've come and asked me. I could've told them about that." It could've happened any time, the way she carried on. All that knocking! And them so drunk! If anything has happened to that young girl, it'll be her fault. If little Rita's hurt or worse, she'll have to take the blame. She wasn't fit to be in charge of a youngster. And she should never have left her by herself, a prey to any undesirables that turned up.'

An hour later, revived by a tuna-fish sandwich and a mug of tea, Olivia sat on her bed and tried to remember all she had heard. Since Stephen had approached her in the library on Monday, the number of people she had met either by chance or intention had multiplied rapidly: four already today and it was only Wednesday afternoon. Their knowledge of Rita ranged from family intimacy to the shop assistant's hearsay, so not all had information and none could assist in the search, but each had at least one comment or opinion about her or where she had lived. It was impossible to estimate their accuracy but, accustomed to studying a play not only for its surface meaning but for the undertones and to discover the line of the sub-text, Olivia examined what she knew.

Discounting for a moment the fanatical convictions of the Dales and Mrs Booth since they defied relation to anything else, she decided that there was some agreement in Steve and Karen's references to Rita's disappearance since he had mentioned that she never stayed long in one place and the latter had inquired whether she had simply bunked off. Both considered her to be reasonably happy where she lived and according to the man in the supermarket she had been looked after well. But the neighbour's account seemed to contradict this and supported Karen's idea that Rita must have been in some trouble since one night she had got drunk. All the details from Karen and Steve were reliable, Olivia decided; she had sensed no dissembling and she could imagine no reason for it. The neighbour's claims, however, were more in doubt. Yet the disorder she had described seemed to fit in with the girl's wrecked bedroom; and that was a fact.

It was the only uncontroversial one she had. Steve had been mystified by the room, she remembered, feeling that there was something wrong with it, but that was unimportant; its state was beyond question. Everything else was a hotchpotch of conjecture and insinuation. These had to be considered cautiously but she could not ignore one feature they shared. Though coming from apparently unconnected sources, they were disturbingly consistent in their references to Elizabeth Drew.

She went through them. The journalist from the *Evening Chronicle* had asked what 'footing' she had enjoyed with Rita and had called her 'that type' and, since Mrs Booth had argued that no landlady would damage a room in her own house, he must have implied that Mrs Drew was responsible; but he would not explain the hint that 'things were going on'. The neighbour had been more explicit; what she had described was probably nothing more than noisy parties occasioning the envious disapproval of a puritanical street, but they had earned Elizabeth Drew a notoriety which had reached the man at the till. This seemed the most sensible explanation but it left her uneasy. Perhaps 'sensible' was not the criterion; it could not encompass Mrs Dale's hope that Elizabeth Drew would get her deserts. Finally, the stooped woman in the shop had been nervous about the police and had thought it had been wise for the other to get away for a while. Which confirmed the neighbour's assumption.

Olivia paused. During the last three days she had listened to voices tuned to anxiety, surprise or irritation, but now they were smothered by others. Sifting through the garrulity of Mrs Booth's report, the neighbour's self-importance, and finding the relevant details, she heard only prejudice and dislike. But for that, she might have been ready to consider the neighbour's accusations, though it was difficult to believe she was seriously claiming that Mrs Drew kept some sort of brothel. The idea was so fantastic that Olivia felt ridiculous applying the word to it, and it was not likely that the neighbour would wait for proof before complaining to the police. Perhaps she was hinting other practices, wife swapping or blue films, for example, secret things not exactly illegal but balanced on the edge of the law. Recalling the woman in the shop, however, Olivia could not imagine her taking part in any such activities.

Again Olivia was perplexed; such a situation was beyond her understanding. Extraordinary, exotic, it was incongruous in that street and her instinct was to reject it. Yet was it so bizarre? Though hardly a regular feature of small-town society, it happened. It was more comprehensible than Mrs Booth's revelation. When she had embarked on the search for Rita she had not expected anything like this.

Above her in the hall the telephone began ringing.

She was tempted to leave it but professional habit was too strong.

'I've been trying to reach you all week but you've been out or engaged,' her mother complained. 'Now calls are being intercepted. Whatever is going on?

'How disgusting! Are you all right, dear? Were they obscene?' Mrs Quinn gabbled after Olivia's explanation.

She answered, congratulating herself on her patience.

'But why should anyone decide to upset you in this way?'

'I'm not upset, Mother. The number has been chosen at random.'

'I hope you're right; but you can't be sure, so I should take precautions.'

'Mrs Winterton already has, as you'll have gathered.'

'I don't mean reporting it to the exchange. I mean being careful. You never know what some people will get up to. If you go out at night you really shouldn't walk back by yourself.'

'Please don't fuss.' Were she to tramp at midday over a ploughed field her mother would warn that the furrows were populated by brigands. 'I've told you – the calls are not directed at me.' She made the insistence so positive that she was almost convinced.

'Very probably not, but you can't depend on it,' the other was equally insistent. 'There are some very strange people about, Olivia.' She didn't know the half of it. 'So you'd be advised not to take chances. Have I ever told you about your father's cousin Gillian?'

'I expect so.'

'She married a few years after us but we couldn't attend the wedding because you had the measles. Well, immediately she and Alex returned from their honeymoon, the telephone calls started. In the middle of the night. They couldn't get a wink of sleep and the moment they answered it, the person cut off. It went on for weeks. Then they put the Post Office on to it and it

79

stopped. Years later the mystery was solved. Somebody sharing digs with the person at the time told Gillian. And do you know who the caller was?'

Her sense of drama is predictable, Olivia thought. But it worked. 'As a matter of fact, no; I don't.'

'An ex-girlfriend of Alex.'

'That's incredible!' For the first time her voice was warm, interested. 'Fancy going to all that trouble! She must have disturbed her own sleep as well. I'd have to be far gone before I did that.'

'Hell knows no fury like a woman scorned,' Mrs Quinn answered, pleased with the quotation. 'You see, she couldn't bear the thought of Alex . . .'

'I get the picture,' Olivia interrupted. 'Has anything of note happened your end since you last phoned?'

'No, I'm afraid not. We live a very quiet life, the two of us,' suggesting riotous revels when there had been three. 'I wanted to tell you how much we enjoyed the programme.'

She couldn't mean that.

'Seeing you on television,' she corrected, rightly interpreting her daughter's silence. 'Have there been any comments?'

'Not as far as I know.'

'I wouldn't be surprised if some director has seen it and has you stored in his mind. We all know that getting your face on television is half the battle.' She had learnt her part well. 'I've been thinking how that must affect you. It must be exciting to go out and have everyone recognize you.'

If her name were up in lights on Shaftesbury Avenue, her mother would bribe the management to keep them switched on during the day.

'Of course everyone has not recognized me, Mother. You talk as if I'd had a star part! And those that have mentioned it have confused me with the woman herself.'

'Surely that's a great compliment! It shows you were very convincing, Olivia, which must give you a lot of satisfaction. I'm delighted. Does this mean that you are meeting a few people? Apart from the others at the agency, you seem to know hardly anyone. One can be very isolated in a new town but if you get to know only a handful of people, you soon feel less miserable.' Her mother's universal cure prescribed for all disorders from compulsive eating to tics. Olivia wished she could contradict it without reservation.

'I don't know how you've formed the impression that I'm miserable. And I'm not a stranger at all; I know dozens of people. There's a fellow called Steve I see every Monday in the library hunting through the Situations Vacant. He's not a boyfriend,' she stated to discourage, 'but we look out for things for each other; and there are all the gossips in the local supermarket where I'm well in with the manager; and there's a couple who invite me to their house – they've a fascinating old mother living with them; and there's Mrs Winterton and neighbours. I could spend my time, if I wanted, just going the rounds. For example, I'm meeting a friend, Karen, in a pub this evening and since others will quickly gather we're bound to have a good time.'

'I'm pleased you've settled in so well. I hadn't realized. But don't forget: whenever you want to get away from it all,' Mrs Quinn said without sarcasm, 'your bed's always made up.'

They had said their farewells and replaced handsets before Olivia recalled that she had not mentioned the audition at the Piccolo Theatre.

Chapter Six

In the Gate, by the market, the peremptory thirsts of the first hour had been quenched and there was a lull for consolidation before the last frenzied provision against the overnight drought. This gave leisure for expressionless scrutiny of a newcomer and heads, swivelled at Olivia's entrance, creaked back to follow her walk to the bar. Not altogether displeased at commanding this public attention which with a little effort could be likened to an appearance on stage, she smiled at the nearest rank of customers and, quickly assessing the form, ordered half a pint of the local brew.

'That'll put some muscle on you,' the barman approved, his position requiring a civility not attempted by others for he added, 'Josh, give the lady a bit of room.'

Josh leant a grudging inch nearer his companion. His back, broad as a door, had been swung in her face when she reached him and she had to squeeze round it to pay and pick up her glass. Almost brushing the grey nylon shirt wealed by the rhombus pattern of the string vest, she flinched nervous, dismayed that she had come.

This surprised her. Though she rarely went into a public house unescorted, she was accustomed to visiting other places alone and had frequently scorned more dependent women who relied upon a companion's shelter, but now she had an intimation of their fear. Standing by the bar, sipping her drink with the convincing poise gained from her training and temperament, she knew that the cold glass slipped and, putting it down, wiped her clammy palm. Across the room, faces, every one male, regarded her; a few were indifferent, others puzzled, some ostentatiously calculating her aggregate of sexual points, all placing her as that other, the woman who had dared to intrude on their patch. Without intention she had challenged a code which admitted women only on sufferance, as invisible appendages of men. Even so, they were not openly hostile. They didn't need to be, she thought, because they had an impromptu champion: Josh.

His face distorted by a look which came near to revulsion, he was watching her image in the mirror behind the bar and as she attempted to lift her glass he leant sideways, pinioning her against the next customer, using his great back as a wedge and crushing her breasts. Still holding this position, he bent his neck towards his companion and said something which drew an answering obscenity. At this they both spluttered, then jetted out vapours of beer and showered spittle in loud mocking hoots.

'Let's hear it, Josh,' the barman pleaded.

'Some other time, Bob, when it's your missis' night off,' offering a slight acknowledgement to a woman replenishing the stock of crisps while giving a sideways nod towards Olivia. Again his eyes scratched down her reflection, and nudged, his friend shared his jeers.

Clamped against the bar, the beer welling vomit in her throat, Olivia felt the panic of something trapped, the desperation of someone cornered in an alley watching the relentless approach of boots that will soon bruise and break. She put down her glass again and began to edge back but, trembling, caught her heel against the leg of a stool. As she apologized to the man who occupied it, she saw across the broad back the leer on the mirrored face. And suddenly defeat was vanquished by anger. She raised a hand, tapped the mocking shoulder and, as the head screwed round, demanded in a voice that

83

carried the length of the bar, 'If you have any remark to make about me, would you please say it to my face.'

The silence was immediate; a few residual echoes tinkled like ice against glass; shocked faces bobbed on the perimeter of her vision but at its centre was his, at first fourteen inches from her own, then six. The eyes jerked among those behind her, recruiting uncritical support, while damp, tufted nostrils distended and the lips drew back over nicotine-grained teeth.

'What's up wi'yer? I've no "remark" to make on you. Don't push yourself. If business is slack, then get outside and wait. Only, I'm fussy, so I'd need a few more inside me first.'

Hedged by a swell of sniggers, Olivia dredged for breath and, with it, words; but another voice said, 'Hi! We've only just seen you. We're round the other side.'

'You've forgotten your drink,' Stephen added, while groping as through a mist she began to follow.

Obediently she went back; the barman pushed her glass towards her; and as she sensed an apology in his gesture, some of her composure returned. She glanced round the circle, still silent, like that one on the telephone who for four days had waited for her to break. And drawing herself up, she looked down at the carious mouth, the clogged nostrils, and keeping her expression calm and lips steady she stared into the eyes until, their triumph faltering, they blinked and slid away.

When she rejoined him, Stephen fussed, 'I hope you haven't been waiting long, but you seem to have struck up a conversation, more than I could manage.' This indicated that he was oblivious of what had occurred and, its repulsive scum still on her, she had no wish to disabuse him. Leading her down two steps and into what must once have been the back parlour, he added, 'They're a rough lot in the bar. In here's more select.'

'Listen to him,' Karen exclaimed, and made a space for Olivia on the bench. 'It's so select you have to be on sup. ben. to get in. She's an actress,' she told the rest, 'with no job. So she can have a free pass.'

'Do you know Meryl Streep?' one asked.

'She's Nick's pin-up for the moment,' Karen explained.

'I'm sorry, no; I haven't met her.'

Nick frowned, disappointed. 'I suppose it was a long shot.'

'There are a lot of us about.'

'You're the first one I've spoke to,' another commented.

'Ask her for her autograph, then, Wayne,' Karen suggested. 'But Trudi's sister's been in a picture, hasn't she, Trudi?'

'Anybody could've been! I could've got a hitch there, no hassle, only they didn't want blokes. Dinner and thirty quid a day! Just for standing in a queue outside a butcher's!'

'What was it?' Olivia asked.

'It was something about a pig, wasn't it, Trudi?' Karen prompted.

'Yes; and they dressed them up old-fashioned. Bet had to wear curlers and a head scarf. She wouldn't have done it if she'd known that first off. She would've died if anyone had seen her.'

'Wayne wouldn't have said no to curlers and a head scarf, would you?' Nick said.

'I wouldn't say no to a bikini for thirty quid.'

'Is there anything you'd say no to, Olivia?' Stephen asked.

'Not a lot. If I had the chance of some work in film I'd take it.'

'Who wouldn't, for thirty quid a day,' Wayne agreed.

'As a matter of fact, I'd hope to get more. You've described work as extras.' She explained, choosing the words carefully in order not to pull rank or put down Trudi's sister.

'It's the difference between professional and amateur,' Stephen concluded, proving as often happened that Olivia's tact was unnecessary.

'You must be rolling,' Wayne admired.

'I would be if I could earn that every day.'

'You have to look at it like this,' Karen interpreted. 'She might do a part then have nothing for weeks. Isn't that right, Olivia? So she has to stash some of it away.'

'And she hasn't actually got a part in a film at the moment,' Stephen pointed out and they all laughed.

'Anyway, I'm more interested in the theatre.'

'Pays better, does it?'

'Wayne, you are awful!'

'Not likely. I barely clear a hundred a week.'

'That's not much of a catch if you can't rely on it,' he commiserated. 'Have you ever thought of television? There must be money in that.'

Eager to establish her association with a star, Karen reported, 'She was on the telly last week, weren't you, Olivia? She told me.'

Wayne opened his mouth but before he could inquire the fee, Olivia said, 'That's why I'm here.'

None of them had seen 'Mystery of the Week', though after Olivia's description Nick told her he was sorry to have missed it, his regret expressed with a fervour that suggested his adoration of Meryl Streep was under siege. Neither could any of them remember when they had last seen Rita.

'Probably not since that night she got pissed,' Wayne tried to calculate. 'Have we? I can't be sure.'

'I don't think so,' Nick agreed.

'Mind you,' Trudi pointed out, 'she could be here all evening and you'd hardly notice. But that time was different.'

'It wasn't only different; it was unique! Most times you sit here spinning out half a shandy, but she was loaded. Drinks all round. No sooner through one than she was shouting for another lot. I was so sloshed I couldn't get up till Mum got back from work next day.'

'So what's new, Wayne?'

'Because I got sloshed. That's what's new.'

'Give over. Your stinking hangover is of no interest to Olivia.'

'It wasn't a stinking hangover. Painful, I grant, but I loved every minute of it. I lay there saying to myself: Enjoy it, man, let yourself enjoy it; it could be years, or never, before you're laid out with another like this.'

'To hear him talk anybody 'ud think nobody else is skint. And it's Rita that Olivia wants to hear about,' Karen, mistress of ceremonies, reminded them.

'Are you really looking for her?' Nick asked.

She nodded, thinking: at the end of this, he's going to ask me out. And warmed by the thought, she discovered that the sickness of the bar had at last drained from her throat.

'I knew she was missing,' Trudi announced, 'because of that in the paper.'

'Both her neighbour and grandmother have mentioned that, but I haven't seen the report.'

'Has she a grandma as well?' Karen asked.

'As well as who? Most people have, or have had.'

'As well as her mum, of course. You *know*, Wayne. And she was enough.'

'She means a real cow,' Trudi interpreted.

Disapproving, Stephen glanced at Olivia and blushed. 'Rita never called her that.'

'Well, she wouldn't, would she? She never stood up for herself.' But she did on the day she left home, Olivia thought. 'You wouldn't catch me putting up with what she did.'

'What sort of thing?'

Trudi shrugged. 'Oh, you know – questions every five minutes, being in when they said.' She floundered, aware that she was enumerating the sins of all parents.

Then recalling some peculiar to Rita's, she added more confidently: 'Her mum was in here once nosing about, asking where she lived. I didn't split on her; not that I knew anyway. And another thing – one night she locked Rita out.'

'That was her dad,' Nick corrected.

'Her stepdad.'

'He can't have been. They had the same name.'

'He was her stepdad, I tell you,' Karen insisted. 'Rita wrote another name once on a book in junior school; I can't remember what it was. The teacher said she had to write what her mother had put when she brought her in. I said to her, you do as you like, but she wouldn't.'

This appeared to confirm Trudi's description.

'It's strange what you learn,' Stephen reflected, twirling his glass. 'Rita never told me that.'

'Kept things to herself.'

'All the same.'

Arrested, their animation stilled, they looked at him. Then Karen glanced towards Wayne, leant across and whispered, 'I expect she would have told you, Steve, when – you know – she thought it mattered.'

Consolatory, the rest murmured agreement, recognizing an affection they had not previously noted though puzzled that the girl's secrecy, of no moment within their casual companionship, should give such pain. And Olivia thought: It is symptomatic of her temperament, that face sulking into the camera, the taciturn member of this group. It was Rita's right to conceal what she wished, yet that could cause distress, just as her leaving home – an unexpected bid for independence – had brought grief. In the interests of our own needs, how far are we justified in ignoring others? she wondered; and with a sudden remorse thought of her mother.

Conscious that he was required to relieve their silence, Stephen mumbled, 'Perhaps Rita doesn't want anyone to look for her.'

'Provided that she's safe. That's what I'm trying to find out.'

'Anything could have happened to her,' Trudi stated, not entirely without relish.

Karen tutted, derisive. 'Such as?'

'It was in the *Evening Chronicle*,' the other defended.

'I wish I'd seen this.' She would have done had she been interested enough in the town to buy the local paper. Perhaps Mrs Winterton would have a copy. 'What did it say?'

'Something about violence not being ruled out. I didn't read it. My dad did, though, when we were having tea. They went on about the woman who had the house where she had a bedsit.'

'Mrs Drew.'

'That's right. She's done a bunk, too. They were asking her to come forward.'

'She'll be daft if she does.'

'But Wayne, they're *asking*!'

'So what? Just look at it her way.' He cleared his throat in preparation for showing them the way Elizabeth Drew could look at it. 'There's been violence, hasn't there? So . . .'

'Not necessarily. Trudi said it hasn't been ruled out. Why did they put that?' Nick asked.

'Rita's room was turned upside down,' Stephen told him.

'Right,' Wayne resumed quickly. 'There's been a fight. First person the fuzz can lay their hands on – he, or she, is for it. Mrs Drew's cleared out, so she's the first suspect.'

'That's ridiculous; I know. I've met her, when I used to visit Rita.'

'I'm not suggesting she was mixed up in it, necessarily. I'm just saying that if there's been a fight she'd be advised to scram, sharpish. She stay around, and the boys in blue will be on her for sure. All they're interested in is making a charge. Remember our Al? He got caught riding a bike without a licence when he was fifteen. After that, they never let up. Any complaint, first thing they did was grab Al: shop-window broken – pull in Al; a fight – fetch Al; kids smoking grass – our Al must have shoved them it. In the end our dad went down to the station and told them if it didn't stop he'd shop a few of them. Knew enough to get some of them inside for life. So if this Mrs Drew's got any sense she'll stay out of the way for a bit.'

'I take your point but I can't imagine a landlady thinking like that.' Yet the woman in the supermarket had feared police interference and had considered Elizabeth Drew wise to get away. 'Can you imagine it?' she appealed to Stephen.

'Not Mrs Drew.'

'You're assuming that the room was done over before Mrs Drew left,' Nick addressed Wayne.

'I've met a neighbour; she noticed that the milk hadn't been taken in and deduced that Mrs Drew left a short time before Rita since she would have remembered to cancel it.' Olivia decided not to introduce the red herring of the knocking men.

'She could be right, but the timing ought to be cleared up. If the room was turned over after Mrs Drew left, then she's in the clear. All the same, I don't agree that it would be intelligent for her to stay out of the way. That would make it look as if she knew something about it and you couldn't blame the police if they suspected she was implicated.'

'Nick's talking sense. But this could have occurred after they had both gone,' Stephen argued. 'It could have been a straightforward burglary. That's what it looked like on Pennine News.'

'I took it for granted that was what it was, at first,' Olivia agreed; 'but the programme wasn't explicit. It didn't say that it was a break-in and apparently the newspaper doesn't suggest that as a possibility.'

'They must have eliminated that, then,' Wayne concluded. 'Maybe this Mrs Drew did it herself.'

'Leave off, Wayne! I've met her. She was slim, and young. I wouldn't say more than about twenty-two.'

'Looking like Olivia?' Nick admired.

'Only when Olivia's not talking. Mrs Drew has the same sort of features but they are less defined. She was – it's difficult to describe – pulled down, somehow, and quiet and shy.'

'You couldn't say that I'm any of those.'

They laughed. 'You wouldn't stick us for long if you were,' one expressed a group complacency and Olivia thought: Poor Rita!

Dismissing this view of Mrs Drew's personality, Trudi asked, urgent, 'Do you mean, Wayne, that she might have done Rita in?' and talking over Stephen's appalled objections, 'It said there might have been foul play.'

'*Might* have been. In other words, they know nothing and they're just providing some sensational reading for people like you,' Nick rebuked.

'Look, *I* didn't read it, did I? It was my dad. And people do get murdered, especially young women. That's not my fault. For all we know, that Mrs Drew might have clobbered her and stuck her in the canal.'

'Or it could have been her stepdad,' Karen suggested. 'For her money.'

Deflected, the other repeated, 'For her money?'

'Yeah. It's often money, isn't it? It 'ud be like this,' ignoring the incipient giggles. 'Rita's stepdad finds out that her proper dad has died and was loaded. He's left her everything, but it's to go to her mum if Rita pops off first. Now her stepdad knows he'll never get a handout from Rita because once he locked the door on her and he calculates that it's on the cards he'll kick the bucket before her. So, wanting to have a chance of a good binge

91

while he's still capable, he gets in his car one night, forces himself into Rita's bedsit, gags her, breaks the place up to make it look like Mrs Drew done it, shoves Rita in the boot, drives to the canal and throws her in. You were right about the canal, Trudi. It's so mucky the Council 'ud be ashamed to have it dragged.'

Flushing, the other tried sarcasm to moderate the applause. 'You shouldn't be wasting time with us; you should be writing detective stories.'

'If I did, I wouldn't come to you for plots.'

'And I wouldn't read them.'

'No. You'd leave that to your dad, wouldn't you?'

'Look, he's not responsible for what goes in the paper. All he said was, if there's talk about foul play then there must be something in it. It was Wayne said maybe Mrs Drew did it herself.'

Their noise was attracting attention. Customers passing the doorway paused to listen, were stared out and then went on. While Olivia recalled Mrs Booth's account of the journalist's visit. He had learnt nothing from them to add to the one concrete fact that he already had: the state of Rita's room; but he had implied fears for her safety. From which it appeared he had fabricated a report to titillate the readers' armchair taste for blood. Again Olivia regretted that she had not bought the local paper. Since she was looking for a girl in one of the towns it covered, she should keep up with its news.

Wayne, either to circumvent mockery or to assert the truth, was insisting that his idea had been misinterpreted. 'I meant, did over Rita's place herself. That night Rita had all that lolly: perhaps she pinched it, then cleared out, and Mrs Drew was doing the place over to see if she could find anything to prove she had.'

'That's a terrible thing to say. Rita isn't a thief.'

'Look, Steve, I didn't say that to get at her but we can't afford to be soft about it. We're trying to find out where she's gone or what's happened to her and for starters we have to know why. It's the only way. If she did pinch the money, then she would have a reason, like wanting to do a bunk. It doesn't make her a thief, not in so many words.'

'All right, suppose we accept that,' Nick came in; 'it doesn't explain why Mrs Drew's gone off as well.'

'That could be just chance.' Speaking more loudly than was needed, Trudi redeemed previous blunders by this emphasis on logic. 'She might've gone away for something else, something that had nothing to do with Rita, whether she'd stole money or not.'

'That's right,' he approved. 'Every little thing's not forced to be connected. It's easy to go over the top. This isn't a book; it's something that happened here. Not every small detail has to add up. There are lots you have to throw out. You can't expect everything to have a heavy significance, like,' he cast around for an example, 'like Rita telling me that last time she was here that she was exhausted since she'd been up most of the night.'

'Did she say why?'

'There you are! I told you Olivia would make a good private dick,' Karen complimented her protégée.

'Not directly. I got the impression that it wasn't by choice, though; more like something had been going on and she'd been dragged in. There can't be anything in that, Olivia, surely?'

'Probably not.' But in some measure this corroborated the neighbour's story. Though prurient, busy with scandal, she could not be entirely ignored. 'Can we go back to that evening Rita got drunk? Let's forget about the money for a moment and concentrate on her. For example, her mood.'

'She was all right. Anybody would be, wouldn't they, with a purseful like that? Not mean with it, either.'

'I don't think she was all right,' Stephen said.

Karen agreed. 'Wayne reckons that if anybody is throwing their money about they're having a good time.'

'Well, wasn't she? There was nothing stopping her. She was here with us, standing the drinks, enjoying herself for once. It was like a party, nicer because it wasn't expected.'

'On Monday when Karen and I ran into each other, she told me that Rita had been upset.'

The other nodded. 'It seemed to me she was trying to shut something off. It wasn't natural, her letting herself go like that. What do you think, Trudi?'

'I thought it was creepy at first, but then I didn't notice much after a bit.' They giggled. 'I remember, though, going down to the lav and she came with me. I stood by the basin and waited while she went in first. I think that's right, but I wouldn't swear to it; I was already half cut. Then she came out and she hadn't been able to do up her zip – she was wearing denims – so I had a go. It took me hours, or felt like it, because the teeth were caught in her pants and I said something like, "Anybody coming in now, Rita, would get the wrong idea." It was the daft sort of thing you say, you know – mumbling on to help the time pass, not trying to get a laugh. But it did. It practically laid her out. She was so creased up, I couldn't go on fiddling with the zip. Only it wasn't nice laughing. It was more like hysterics and I did wonder whether I ought to give her a slap on the face. I didn't because I didn't like to and because she was crying as well, with the laughs, until gradually it got worse and she was just crying. When she stopped I wet a paper towel and dabbed at her face and lent her my powder. I had to put that on for her as well. When we got back I realized that I hadn't used the loo.'

'She must have been more drunk than I realized,' Nick commented.

'I don't think she was, then. It was creepy. I didn't like it.'

'Soon drowned your sorrows,' Wayne laughed.

But the rest were puzzled, their expressions sombre, and as the barman in the adjacent room called for last orders they raised their glasses and sipped the last drops.

'She'd hurt her wrist,' Karen recalled suddenly. 'That 'ud be why you had to help her with the zip. When we were going out she tripped up the step. I grabbed her and she let out such a yell! "My wrist got twisted," she said because I asked. "I'm not generally that clumsy." Afterwards it came to me that she must have been referring to that glass she knocked over. She must have been using her left hand.'

'She didn't mention any injury,' Stephen muttered, 'though I took her home. As far as the gate.'

While Olivia, listening to the ambiguity of 'got twisted', connected it with Nick's deduction that there had been an incident when Rita was 'dragged in'. Suddenly the talk round her seemed irrelevant. 'I must be going,' she said.

'Keep in touch,' Karen grinned. 'You know where to find us.'

'I'll come with you. There's something . . .'

Disappointed that Stephen's offer had preceded his, Nick asked, 'Are you on the phone? So we can give you a ring if there's anything else.'

'And you give us a buzz if you're on to anything,' Wayne said. 'You can count us in.'

Their voices clacked round her. Their upturned faces were featureless discs receding before the image of a hand gripping, screwing a young girl's arm. She reached out, urgent to save. 'I'll give Steve my number,' she promised them.

'I didn't like to introduce this in front of them, knowing what they would make of it,' Stephen began when they were outside; 'but I've got a key to Mrs Drew's house.

Rita give it to me that night, saying that any time I wished I could let myself in. I refused it because I couldn't imagine such an occasion but she wouldn't listen. She was so determined I should have it, I took it in the end just to satisfy her. Frankly I found it rather ironical to be given a key to a house I no longer visited. Probably the only occasion in my life it'll happen, too; and useless.'

'You could quote it in the future as customary procedure.'

'Some hope! But I'm telling you because, if you ever want to have a look round, that's possible.' He stopped under a lamp, found a diary and scrawled a telephone number. 'Here,' tearing out the page, 'and shall I take yours? Nick thought that advisable,' he reminded her, shyness requiring another's authority to make the request.

She dictated her number but did not tell him that it was monitored. She had no desire to cause Stephen to worry for her.

They walked on, talking about what had been said, but afterwards she could remember nothing of this conversation, gentle and almost elegiac in the amber light, because of Josh.

He had come upon her as she walked towards the lavatory, Stephen having gone ahead to wait in the street, and barring her way had snarled, 'Don't think you can get away with it, you bitch. I've about had a bellyful and I'm not standing for any more.'

Forced against the wall, she saw a hand swing then drop as heels clattered on slate slabs.

'Night, Josh,' the bartender's wife dismissed him. 'See you tomorrow. After you, love,' holding open the door for Olivia.

Cramming damp paper towels into a plastic bag, she asked, pretending casualness, 'Are you all right, love? You look a bit peaky.'

'It's nothing. I need to get to bed.'

'There isn't much that doesn't cure. But if that Josh said anything to you, don't you take no notice. He's not my cup of tea, I admit, but there are circumstances. His wife's forever leaving him. He'll fetch her back, then she'll go off again. Sometimes I think you can't really blame her, but it was her married him and she ought to stick to it. She owes him that. A man loses his self-respect when he can't keep hold of his wife.'

And when does a woman lose hers? Olivia thought.

Chapter Seven

With sixteen members in the agency and seven at present in work, the rota changed each fortnight and Olivia was on duty Thursday that week. The morning was lambent with colour, encouraging economy on bus fares and prompting a sense of release. Pausing to buy apples at an open market, Olivia was salved by the dreamless light and the sun's unguent on her flesh. The hours ahead at typewriter and telephone would be busy but peaceful, and the thought of them relieved the crush of the man's chest and suppressed the threat of his fist; suppling her movements and brightening her face. Neither was any of this diminished when Dora Booth joined her by the stall.

'You're up in good time,' she greeted.

'It's my turn at the office.' She explained. 'We've taken some space in Crimple Mill.'

'That's a fair walk. Nice early on, mind you, but wearisome after a day in the sheds. I was there, start of the war, then it went in for munitions. A fine let-down, that, after weaving.'

'You'd hardly guess at either, now. It's been divided into what are called compact units to rent. In other words, microscopic, but we don't need much space. On the first floor there's the main office of a travel agency, a couple who make soft toys, a restaurant, a woman who designs posters, and us.'

Mrs Booth sneered. 'Come to a pretty pass, hasn't it, when a mill that used to turn out thousands of bolts a week is filled with folk doing nothing useful.'

'I hadn't considered that,' she admitted, though she would have expressed the change in political terms.

'You haven't seen as many years as me.'

The stallholder proffered the apples and waited for payment. Olivia searched for the correct change, hoping that Mrs Booth would accept her concentration as a signal to part. But was disappointed.

'I've been thinking about you. There's something that should have been said,' she told Olivia abruptly. 'I didn't know he hadn't, till you'd gone, second time. It's not my business, looked at any road up, but I said to Charlotte, she's owed it; the young woman should know why he was after seeing her. You were round in the afternoon, Monday, weren't you? And that man from the *Evening Chronicle* came in the morning. It was because of that.'

'Mr Dale wished to see me because a journalist had visited you?'

'That's right. He's got more up on top than Charlotte, though I'm her mother that says it, and he had his suspicions what might come of it, so he wanted to tell you there was nothing personal.'

'How could there be anything personal – anything related to me? We hadn't even met!'

'They'd seen you on the telly.'

'But representing someone else. Mr and Mrs Dale knew nothing about me, *myself*.' And no more about Elizabeth Drew. 'I haven't seen the report but I know that violence was mentioned. They could hardly suggest that I was responsible for that, if there were any.' She giggled; their confusion was so ridiculous.

'That's finished, then. You don't sound to have been put to any inconvenience.' However she did not move away.

'I must get on. I'd like the chance to open the post before the telephone starts ringing,' smiling to herself because today, in the office, the handset would not slip

99

in her palm. She could not convince herself that the exchange's interception was foolproof.

'Yes; it's a fair walk,' the other repeated. Then thrusting her basket against Olivia's legs, 'If you do come across Rita, you tell her that her grandma's found out. It's taken a bit of time but she knows now and she'll be round her quick if she doesn't shift herself, the sly little madam. You tell her it's the last thing I'd have imagined coming from her. I've never been so disgusted, but I'll undertake not to bring her mum into it if she comes and tells me.'

Pinned against the market stall, disconcerted as she'd been at their previous meeting by a swift change of tone, Olivia saw that the annoyance and disgust were less important than the emotion they concealed. For the woman was no longer spry, a sexagenarian in energetic health; she was old and ill, her cheeks rusted and flaking, dry as if the juice of her life had drained off.

'Yes, I'll tell her, if I find her,' she agreed, pushed the basket aside and walked quickly up the street.

'She's round the twist,' she reminded herself; 'absolutely barmy,' trying to forget the desolation in the woman's face. 'They all are. Like her daughter Charlotte's, her speech is maniacal. They string words together in an intelligible sequence but the sense is malformed. It means nothing. They talk in riddles as if trying not to admit to themselves what it is they are saying. You could call it the sub-text, except there's no text for this to be sub!'

Enlivened by this notion, she stepped into the pavement's sunny border and strode among early shoppers whose expressions were matched to the routine business pursued. Terrors, follies, passions were undisclosed and, choosing not to doubt the crowd's public face, Olivia accepted its ordinariness with relief, turning her memory from the one that remained by the stall. 'I'll think about it later,' she promised herself. 'There's no time for that today. Which I hope will give me plenty to do but which will certainly be uncomplicated. A rest from the Dales.'

She raised her face to the light, invited back her former contentment and, ignoring litter, dust and spent buildings, she willed herself into a holiday mood as she walked through a car-park and along decaying streets towards Crimple Mill.

The first three hours were as occupied as she had hoped – hoped because activity increased the chance of engagements. Already ringing as she entered the office, the telephone was not an enemy but an ally humming goodwill. She wrote down the details of this availability check, telephoned the actor, declined with stagey sighs his equally stagey invitation to join him in bed, and reported back to the casting assistant. She followed up two inquiries from a maker of commercials and another from Northern Video Productions who were looking for a plump, unexceptional-looking (!) actress in her thirties to lend credibility to a nursery-nurse training film. She read the previous day's entries in the log book and chased a television director through a phalanx of minions to announce that the agency had just the man for a part and solicit an interview. She scanned the sheets from the Script Breakdown Service that had arrived that morning, underlined forthcoming productions with parts suitable for colleagues, and began on introductory letters. Copying out a theatre's address, she noticed that BBC 2 was planning to dramatize *Moll Flanders* and, to anticipate their search for a cast, she telephoned the library to ask them to reserve the book. Returning to the letters, she discovered they had run out of photographs of one of their members so she switched on the answering machine, locked up and ran out to order another set of prints. Ten minutes later, back in the office, she found a request on the machine to phone Alnwick. She did so. They were offering Earl a part, and

101

as soon as the line was clear again she was pressing out his number, delighted to be the one to give him the news. But there was no answer and feeling like a child trusted with a secret but bursting to tell, she left the desk, filled the kettle at the tap in the corridor and brewed herself tea.

She opened the letters delivered in the second post and was puzzling over a cheque for their 'Mystery of the Week' engagement from which it appeared that Alan had been paid more than herself, when she was interrupted.

'Look what I found lurking on the stairs,' Earl greeted, dragging in Raymond. 'With felonious intent.'

'I have to live up to my reputation. I started painting one of my outsides this morning, then the customer went shopping and put all the windows on the latch, so I've knocked off for a beer.'

'We're not licensed,' she told him.

'I know. That'll have to be remedied. I shall bring it up at the next meeting. Normally when I'm on shift I fetch in a couple of cans. I'll not stay long. How's tricks?'

'I'll not take my coat off; I'm not stopping,' Earl mimicked the accent.

'He's got a job.'

From the evidence of the next minutes, an onlooker would have deduced that Olivia had offered it. She was embraced, kissed, danced and whirled in the air. 'A good thing this doesn't happen every day. I'm getting past it,' Raymond wheezed as he dropped her to the floor. Then, 'Let me be the first to congratulate you, Earl. You deserve it,' and resorting to the formality of his generation, he grabbed the other's hand.

'Now look, you've embarrassed him. He's blushing under the soot.'

Again they were laughing; and as they discussed the company's season, the tour of theatres and halls scattered over the lovely Northumberland fells, the plans to attend performances, they were clamorous, exultant, partners in triumph. This party mood seduced them to optimism about Olivia's forthcoming audition and it informed their comments on her search for Rita Dale.

'Now don't you neglect the learning for that test,' Raymond advised.

'I don't have to learn anything specially for it, just polish up my regular pieces.'

'We'll have to coach Raymond in a few. All he's experienced so far is interviews. He hasn't suffered an audition.'

'It's my face they want.'

'Lucky that's the limit of their desires, Ray, because we certainly should have trouble persuading them you haven't got defective vision.'

'You know about that little misunderstanding, Olivia? I'd got this notion he'd be like a young lad I used to play with down our street – he'll be a grown man now – and I was looking out for him. It's easy for an idea to get fixed. And what I'm saying is, you ought not to get wrapped up in looking for that girl,' he continued without a pause to indicate a change of subject. 'It's a job for the Constabulary. Earl remarked that you were seeing some of her mates. What did they have to say about it?'

'They really went to town on it, when they could keep to the point.' She recounted their conversation.

'That's codswallop! Murder!'

'The stepfather theory wasn't serious, Raymond.'

'I'm pleased to hear one of them had some sense. If that had been on the cards, they wouldn't have let it on to the telly without more caution. Believe me, all that's happened is that young lass has nipped off, probably pinching something on the way out. Nothing very remarkable.'

Olivia did not rouse herself to invite an explanation for the wrecked room, nor did she mention Rita's sprained wrist, her crying in the lavatory, her reference to a sleepless night. Warmed by the sun's stroke through the polished glass and sleeked by Earl's good fortune, she felt lazy and disinclined to resume the questions of the last three days.

And when Earl said, 'That sounds plausible enough, Olivia,' she did not remind him that plausibility was concerned with appearances, not truth.

'You don't have to prove her dad wrong,' he insisted.

It was a second before she understood. There had been so many accounts, hints and guesses since their hamburger on Tuesday evening that he was out of date. 'No; I can leave her mother to do that. But I should like to know why she went. Karen said she thought Rita was happy until recently. In spite of the goings-on at the house, described by the neighbour.'

'So there's a knocking shop on Hackney Street!' Raymond gasped through hoots when she had finished. 'Next time you've got a tale like that would you mind giving me warning. It's enough to make a chap swallow his false teeth. I must say they've kept it secret. There isn't a body I know has got wind of it. Not even Arthur, and he has all the news *before* it's happened; goes by the look in the eye. I can't wait to see his face when I tell him.'

He rose, leant against the filing cabinet as if it were a bar and, pitching his voice to a circumspect confidence, addressed Earl. 'Here, Arthur, I've got something to tell you. You're not going to like it, I can assure you of that, being as it casts doubt on your standing as the man with the news.'

'I'm big enough to take it.'

'It's not the beer belly that's in question, Arthur, but the heart. I would have said, the mind, but we have to be realistic. It's like this, Arthur. I was up at a house on Hackney Street yesterday, plying my trade with brush and distemper – I still call it that, you know, though it's really that newfangled emulsion – and this old biddy comes with a shovel and clocks me one on the head. "What's that for?" I asked, being of a curious nature and glad I was wearing my helmet, it having a visor, you see, which protects the eyes from the paint. "For keeping us up all night with your knocking," she answers. "Don't think I'm deceived by you painting that gate. I saw you last night as I righted the curtain . . ." '

'And vowed I would give you a thump on your pate,' Earl chanted.

'Do me a favour, will you, Arthur: keep off the poetry and stick to writing jokes. England's Glory number three hundred and sixty-eight, and we don't have to quote it, very near raised a laugh. You go on like that, by the time you reach four figures I reckon you'll be challenging this biddy in the Back Streets Comedy Contest. Except to qualify you have to be round the bend, and you may be on the gullible side, Arthur, but you're not half-baked. I can see you're gagging, so I'll put you out of your misery. Wait for it, Arthur. Take a good grip of that bar. I didn't know it any more than you at the time, but I was painting the red-light district. A bit small, as it turned out, because there's only the one house, but there's room for expansion. Not over this neighbour's fence, though. She's not in favour. So she bangs on the wall. All night they're rolling in, men still in their muck. But not in our class, Arthur. If we were gasmen lodging in Hackney Street and called out, we'd wash us in the Men's before we went back, wouldn't we? Or if we'd done overtime in Hudson's, we'd wipe the grease off before we came in. Or if your missis had fallen out with you – a risk, Arthur, unless you improve on those jokes – and she'd set up in Hackney Street and you reckoned another bloke was there licking the cream, you'd down a few one night and go round with your mates to see him off, wouldn't you? No, looking at you, Arthur, I can see you wouldn't, but there's many that would. And another thing that wouldn't worry you would be her next door

– that is, if you were a gasman or down at the yard – because you wouldn't have time to notice some nosy parker with nothing better to do than stand at the curtains, and with an imagination that 'ud do credit to her hubby's comics. But I can guarantee you one thing, Arthur, if you were a young lass living in that house – you have to force yourself to get inside that – you'd get fed up with it all, now and again, and if your stepdad turned up, as some have the habit when they calculate their daughters are presentable young women and well out of nappies, you'd smile sweetly, take his bribe for affection and blow it in the pub. And you'd do the same if your landlady had a bloke who, to get you out of the way for a couple of hours, handed over a wad. And now, folks, we'll finish with a singalong with Ray, that all-time favourite, "Sonny Boy". A-one, a-two, a-three!'

They had polished off the first verse and were into a deep-throated rendering of the chorus when the telephone sounded.

'I hope that I haven't interrupted a rehearsal, my dear,' Mrs Winterton said, hearing the lingering strains, 'though I was never fond of Al Jolson. Would he have been so successful, do you think, had he been a Negro instead of a white blacked up? Anyway, I'm phoning to tell you that I shall not return from my nephew's this evening but should be back by tomorrow night. So don't forget to lock up if you go out. Have you read what I left you?'

'I didn't see anything.'

'I put it by the phone. Perhaps other things have collected on top of it.'

'I wouldn't be surprised. What is it?'

'Last Monday's *Evening Chronicle*. There's a report on page three that you might like to con. I'm afraid I didn't notice it until I was looking for paper when emptying ashes out of the boiler. I thought you might be interested. And I spoke to the woman at the exchange about those silly calls.'

'Yes. Thank you.'

'I forgot that you would be at the agency today so I telephoned home first. It was a curious feeling being required to quote the number I was phoning when it happened to be my own! Then the request for your name was unexpected, so I stumbled over that. You will appreciate my fears about my sister Dorothy. However, the arrangement was necessary. I must leave you now, but don't grow anxious. I'll be home tomorrow.'

Replacing the handset, Olivia wondered why she should grow anxious.

'That would seem like a natural break,' Earl said. 'Mustn't hold up the good work any longer. Keep cheerful, lovie.' He put his arms around her. 'You pay attention to what our Ray says; he's been around for centuries – that shop-soiled face proves it. He'd make a better sleuth-hound than either of us.' By including himself he reaffirmed his willingness to help her, but with their raucous parody of the song still in her ears and with her wrist circled by his hand, polished aubergine lightening to rose in the palm, her task seemed no longer important.

'Do you really mean better, or a detective with more style? I think Raymond belongs in the Inspector Clouseau category.'

'A brilliant piece of casting! We must remember that, if anything similar comes up. He has a perfect record, having managed to shake hands with the wrong man. You may yet get another job, Raymond! See you later.'

'Was he addressing you or me?' she asked when he had left.

'Both. That's if you're in agreement. Him getting a part calls for a celebration. I'll introduce you to my local; it's the Pig and Whistle. I expect you'll have heard of it. If you board the number eighty at the clock round seven, I'll meet you at the terminus, then I'll fetch you back.

The missis can come, too; it's about time she met a few of you. Sometimes the way she looks I reckon she thinks this agency is another one of my stories.'

'And isn't it? But thanks, it's a lovely idea. I'll buy a sandwich round the corner and join you straight from here.'

'No need for that. I'll stand you a chicken in a basket if you're feeling peckish. Not one of my more sophisticated jokes, that, but it'll pass on a good night. Chicken, you see, Olivia, and peck-ish.'

'I didn't want to egg you on.'

'Not bad, if they got it. When I'm running short of material, I'll give you a ring. I'll be off, then. You know, whoever painted this place out didn't do such a bad job,' he remarked as, standing by the door, he scrutinized the office. 'I'm referring to the workmanship, not the colours.'

They were yellow and purple, fanning like spotlights down the walls and providing bold frames for notices and theatre posters. 'Earl did it.'

'I might have known. It's arty. He's a talented young man.' Raymond hesitated. 'Speaking in confidence you understand, Olivia, I'd like to tell you something. I've kicked around a bit and I'll be forty-five next March, but Earl's been an eye-opener to me. I'm ashamed to admit it because it doesn't reflect well but till I joined here I'd always been hard on his sort. (I'm not talking about his colour.) I took the view of my mates and them in the Clubs. I'm not giving excuses, just saying that I never thought; it was automatic to sneer. Perhaps that was because if we didn't we were feared that we might be taken for the same. I don't know. But I don't see it that way now I've met him, and I want you to know that I'm grateful. There's room for improvement in all of us and I'd not like to think I was too blind to see it or be too stuck to make the change. And there's one thing I'm certain of, something I'll never do again, I can guarantee that. I'll never take them off in the Clubs – you know, pansy, getting an easy laugh. I blush now to think on. I never thought I was being more than just mucky, exciting sniggers at the lengths they go to, doing what they do.'

His final phrase seemed to echo another, but she could not place it immediately and Raymond having confessed to a prejudice was now waiting for her answer, his look nervous.

'That's all right, Ray,' she said inadequately. 'You needn't have told me.'

'I'm one of this outfit now, aren't I? I wanted you to know. Put the record straight.'

'In the circumstances it cannot be entirely that.'

Their seriousness broken, they laughed together. 'There'll always be a word sticking up ready for someone to trip over,' he observed. 'Now don't forget the number eighty leaves from the clock at seven, give or take a few minutes.'

'I'll be on it. And Ray,' she halted his opening the door, 'thanks for the deduction. After the last three days I needed to hear some sense. What you worked out could be a lot nearer the truth than other suggestions.'

'Well, I'm the man on the spot. I know how things happen round here.'

'Anyway, it was good of you to help. I imagine that act would go like a bomb in the Clubs.'

'Bless you, girl, the lads wouldn't like that. Too subtle by far. I can see when it comes to some things your education's not all that it should be. I'll take you round a few. What they want is something broader and jokes they're easy with. Like: "Ta ta for now, then. Be good. But if you can't be good, be careful; and if you can't be careful, buy a pram." '

Refreshed by this interval of company, Olivia finished the letters, went out for a sandwich and paid the telephone bill. Recording this, she was reminded of the

109

cheque from the television company and, after examining the invoice again, decided to inquire why there was a difference in the fees.

'I'm wondering whether there has been a mistake,' she explained to the casting assistant. 'I understood it was an eighty-pound minimum with overtime as a percentage of that. Could you tell me at what point overtime starts? I did the same number of hours as Alan Featherstone but my payment is less.'

'I'm sorry; I should have detailed the fee breakdown. Sloppy of me. I assumed you would recognize the reason. It's quite correct. Mr Featherstone has received the agreed rate for the programme plus an additional fee for the short piece of dialogue which wasn't scripted.'

'Thank you for clearing that up. Alan will be delighted.' She wanted to ask, what unscripted dialogue? But if the company were lavishing cash on film that didn't go out she felt under no obligation to argue.

'To be frank, we didn't intend to use the lines, so you might say that Mr Featherstone is lucky.'

Another riddle-monger! She seemed to attract them. 'You didn't intend to use the lines?'

'Good heavens, no! That was a mistake. The editor had to dash off immediately, so he left a message. Unfortunately it wasn't picked up. Mr Featherstone was asked to improvise a few lines to round off, some appropriate comments to give the reaction of the ordinary man in the street. Anything more might have compromised the director. As it is, that's exactly what has happened. There's been the devil to pay and I'm thankful that I'm well out of it. To be fair, I expect that Mr Featherstone must have thought the camera had stopped rolling after his first remarks, though I consider even those to be questionable. Certainly, though, it was meant to cut all of them. Instead of which, the whole two minutes went out.'

'Thank you for the explanation. I'm sure Alan will be

as sorry as you that things went wrong.' But not enough to contemplate reimbursement. 'Do keep in touch. We're in the middle of designing new CVs to bring us up to date and shall be sending out copies as soon as they're ready.'

So Alan's lines must have come at the end; and the director must be over-reacting to feel compromised by a few lines so mumbled that they couldn't be heard. Except that the director had struck her as very laid back and Alan never mumbled; one of his weaknesses was an incapacity to throw anything away. Then she recalled how she and Judy had mimicked him, had begun to fool about as the credits came up. Perhaps his voice had been over those. She would have to look at the recording again. Since in Rita's room the director had achieved shots that were nearly pornographic, it would be interesting to see what overstepped his tolerance in speech. She could not imagine how this would impugn his discretion or why it was so important. She would watch the recording again, dissociate herself from her own part in it, listen carefully through to the finish, and consider objectively the final effect of a film which did not incriminate her.

But as she made herself a cup of tea before leaving the office, she was surprised to hear the rattle of the spoon against the side of the beaker and though to steady it demanded an effort, she allowed herself to wonder only why she should be so exhausted after a single day's work.

Chapter Eight

Waving goodbye to Raymond, she watched his car slide round the corner before pushing her key into the lock. It had been a jolly evening and her tiredness was healthy as if she had spent a day outdoors. Her body was lithe; skin tingled. Astride the mat in the hall she performed a few exercises, laughing at herself, 'You're drunk.'

But she wasn't; she was happy and she wanted this to continue, was anxious to prevent its passing away from her before it was fully enjoyed. And urgent, she returned to the door, to make into reality the sensation of her hair settling back against her cheeks after wind-blown miles she had not walked, for the only way to do this was to go out again, out of the passage which constricted her, its walls leaning in, its linoleum curling under the brand of the street lamp, its stale air shrinking from the wide night.

The impulse was arrested; the happiness died. She pushed herself away from the door and walked towards the entrance to the basement, admitting that the desire for freedom had been an instinct to escape which she must control, admitting it was panic that contracted the hall, that there was a reason for the draughts, and asking herself what could have stopped her ears against the crunch of glass when she entered the house. Possessed by the certainty, she did not search elsewhere and went down the steps, but laboriously, placing a foot beside the other on each tread before descending to the next in order to delay the moment when she must reach her room.

She let the door bang back and stood on the threshold. She did not go in. It was not hers any more. Her tenancy had been gentle. There was no sign of that now. It was a place gaping and bruised. Undefended, it had cracked open and spilled under the force of another's tearing hand.

Slowly, her legs heavy, she shuffled away from it, took hold of the handrail and pulled herself up the steps. Thinking, 'I can sleep in the kitchen. There's a sofa. I shan't be cold. It's covered by a rug. I can get under that. Nobody will notice.' But at the top of the steps her head screwed round without her volition and her eyes, dragged along the phosphorus shaft, observed its brilliance unhindered by dusty glass, then the empty pane in the door. Remembering, she told herself, 'The person won't come back. Lightning never strikes in the same place twice.' It was a phrase of her mother's and she would have denounced its use but her palate was dry.

In the kitchen she opened a tap and started at the juddering pipes; as she raised a cup, the sound of water slopping on to the draining board lifted through the house. She felt watched, listened to; that the spirit of the intruder was no longer confined to the ruin at the bottom of the steps; and choking on shallow breaths, her flesh rising to cold points, she leant against the sink, shocked by her fear, shocked too by the discovery that against this malignancy she was insufficient and that she must call upon help.

'I'll telephone Earl,' she whispered to herself as she tiptoed into the hall. The thought comforted her. The feel of his arms hooping her to him, the stroke of his fingers in her hair, his permission for tears, cajoled her.

She dialled a number. 'Judy?' she asked.

'Who else? You're lucky. I've only just got in. I'm knackered. The bloody lights fused half an hour before the call and I mislaid three props. Alan tells me you've got an audition. That's brilliant.'

'Judy, will you come?'

'Come? When? I'm likely to be working on Sunday if the first night's anything to go on.'

She had forgotten. 'How was it?'

'Hairy! The director was seen leaving at the interval. You having a party?'

'This isn't a party.'

'Olivia, are you all right?'

'I don't know.'

'You don't sound it.'

'It was silly to phone. You're so far away.'

'I'm here at the end of this line.'

She could not answer. Words stopped at the futility of the hope.

'Olivia? What is it?'

'I shouldn't have phoned. I'm sorry. Being foolish. There's not really anything you can do.'

'Christ! Hang on. Let me think. The last train and coach will have gone, but there's the van and it's not loaded up. Even so, I couldn't be with you in less than an hour and a half. That any good?'

'Oh, Judy . . .'

'Save that. No problems. Except that I'm famished; I haven't eaten since one. So while you wait you can do something useful and throw a few things together.'

'I can't. I can't go into my room.'

'What?'

'It's been turned over. Somebody's broken in.'

There was a hiss of sieved breath then. 'Say an hour and a quarter. It may be no more than fifty miles. Have you telephoned the police?'

'No.'

'Then do that, and don't move anything before they arrive.'

'I shan't. I can't touch it.'

*

'No, I haven't touched anything. I can't,' she repeated, leading him into the kitchen.

'You're a sensible young woman.' He laid down his cap and took out a notebook. 'What time did you get back?'

'I didn't look. It can be only a few minutes ago.'

'Between ten-thirty and eleven sound all right? Any sign of anything at all out of the way when you came in?'

'Only the glass.'

'I meant in the street. But yes, there's no doubt how entry was effected. Better than a notice, Welcome. Leaded lights are easy enough, but a bit of clear glass puttied into the frame! They didn't even need a cutter and could see in to check before they began. I'm sorry, Miss; I know this isn't the right moment for criticism but I do wish people would pay more attention to what we say. A door like that wants something more than a rim-lock on it. All they had to do was get a hand in, see, and turn the knob. But you'll have noticed.'

'Yes.'

'An interest of mine, anti-theft devices. You'll have heard of the Mulholland Bolt? You haven't? Mine. Quite a simple invention. You could have done with one on that door. They're in all the ironmongers and I'm hoping one day they'll get into Woolworths.'

'This isn't my house.'

'But you'll pass on the word? I'll want the name of the owner. The Duty Sergeant said you reported that she's not at home, but before that, let's take a look at the damage.'

'The room's in the basement.'

'That's right,' consulting his notes. 'You must tell me if anything's missing.'

'Could I do that tomorrow?'

He stared at her. 'You've taken this badly, haven't you, Miss? That's not unnatural. Folk do. But it'll wear off, once everything's set to rights,' he consoled, avuncular. 'I reckon tomorrow will suffice. After all, it's late. So I'll go down and examine then you can come into the station in the morning and we'll put in a report. Now you just get that kettle on and make yourself a cup of tea while I go down and see what's what.'

Returning, he tutted, filled the kettle and put it over the gas. 'Here, let's be having that rug that's under you,' he said and draped it round her shoulders. 'You're a right one, you are, sitting there shivering when there's means to be warm. Haven't you heard of First Aid? I hope I'm never knocked down when there's only you passing.'

So he prattled in the manner of a nursemaid distracting a child while he opened cupboards, found Mrs Winterton's tea caddy, sugar bowl and tin of dried milk. 'There's no fresh, so we'll make do with this,' he told her. 'It belongs to the owner, doesn't it? She'll not mind us cadging in an emergency. What's she called?' and, attempting discretion, placed his book on the draining board out of her sight and scribbled down the name. 'It's not the tenant we have to concern ourselves with in the event of a break-in, you see. The owner's the one. It's a question of house insurance, so it's him we have to trace. You'll not believe what a job that can be at times. We're lucky here, your landlady living on the spot. Pity she wasn't at home tonight.

'I'll let the tea stand a few minutes; you'll benefit more from it strong. Then you'll be able to go downstairs and get into bed. Tidying'll keep till the morning. There's nothing broken, Miss, and no other abuse so it's not so bad as it looks at first sight. They'd be after immediate cash because the video-recorder's still there.

'Now what about that for a cup of tea? Strong enough to stand your spoon up in it. I don't fancy one myself, thanks; we've got a new coffee percolator down at the station and I'll help myself to a cup when I get back.

116

There are a number of things I have to mention before I go, Miss. I sent a call out to our Scenes of Crime Officer and he was free to come straight away but, as I expected, there aren't any fingerprints. As far as gloves are concerned, you could say that nowadays burglars are all gents. Kevin washed the dusting powder off when he'd finished; he's a nice lad, is Kev. So we haven't added to the mess. And another thing: since it's too late to get some more glass in, I've fixed a chain though I'm one hundred per cent certain that they'll not be back. You fasten that chain behind me. You must have been wondering what I was up to, hammering and making such a din.'

'No,' she said truthfully because she had not heard.

'Talk about breaking and entering,' Judy said, standing beside her. 'Well, I've entered without breaking in. Gave me quite a buzz. I suppose the chain was some copper's attempt at defence; no good, though, left hanging. Is there any tea left? Heavens, it's stewed. Is that why you haven't drunk it? I must say this isn't much of a welcome. I was expecting some supper.'

And then Judy's arms were round her and a hand was stroking her arm and there were murmurs that did not upbraid the retch of tears.

When she was quieter Judy helped her lie down and covered her with the rug. 'I'll go and clear up.' And Olivia slept.

Sounds woke her, a slithering then a low curse, and finding herself, by the cushions and the patch of window, in the wrong place, her memory hurled back. Sweat slimed her groins and her throat clicked in an attempt to cry out.

'It's OK. Only me,' Judy interpreted. 'I came to see how you are. I've fried eggs and bacon. Four o'clock is rather early for breakfast but the canteen's preparing for the morning shift. I hope you're hungry,' and she switched on the light.

At the top of the stairs Olivia said, 'Smells good,' but hesitated.

'My cooking may be out of this world, ma'am, but my cleaning is miraculous.'

'Is that so?'

'Straight up.'

So she went down the steps and entered the room which was restored now and tranquil. It was hers again. Its blemishes and shortcomings, inherent; its deformities had not been induced. And now her weeping was quieter, an expression of gratitude, while Judy fussed at the stove.

'I've sorted most things out. Those I couldn't find a home for I've stacked behind the settee,' she told Olivia while they ate. 'You'll know if anything's been taken; obviously I can't tell that. But your cheque book's still here and some money in an envelope, so he probably got scared and cleared out. He was a cheeky devil, coming in the front door, but he must have felt quite exposed here at the front.'

'You would expect him to pocket the money, though.' Revived by sleep, her sight not scratched by evidence of his passage, she could look round the mended room and consider what had occurred.

'Not necessarily. He may have intended to take the video-recorder. He'd been playing it, unless you'd left it on. No, I didn't expect you would. I thought he might have been after that sort of thing so I went upstairs to check, but nothing's disturbed in the rest of the house.'

'Mrs Winterton doesn't approve of newfangled machinery.'

'I realized that. I didn't like snooping about but I couldn't help noticing the mangle in the scullery and the meat safe where most of us would have put a fridge.'

'I like it.'

'Yeah. It's cute.'

'So you think he was interested in the video-recorder?'

'Seems like it. Pretty typical, as far as I've gathered. Anyway, something, some noise, stopped him. A good thing it did before you arrived back. I sometimes imagine what I'd do if I were to come across a burglar. I always manage to sock him one before he does me. Which reminds me. I heard from Alma this week. She's touring in *Trafford Tanzi*, lead part.'

'That's marvellous.'

'Isn't it? But also risky. She's thinking of claiming danger money. She had a lot of coaching, of course; they all did. But during rehearsals the chap playing her husband threw her and broke a couple of ribs. It was bloody painful but she says she could put up with that. What she couldn't come to terms with was his clumsiness. This Fandangle Cob only got the part because he's done some wrestling and he was so enthusiastic he kept forgetting it wasn't a proper ring, though even there the bouts are faked. She's furious. You know what Alma's like. She can't forgive him for being so unprofessional and says she's thankful they weren't in a thriller in which he had to bump her off, otherwise she'd be communicating by a medium. But she's determined to pay him back. Now she's playing the scenes with him for real and guarantees he'll have at least two broken ribs by the end of the tour.'

They laughed. 'So much for Alma's professionalism.'

'That's what I thought.'

'I would have benefited from some coaching in wrestling this week,' and she told Judy about the man in Greasy Len's. 'There was another man, too, called Josh,' and to recount his molesting her, she had to explain her reason for being at the Gate and describe her search.

When she was half-way through, Judy called for an interval while she made coffee: 'Gallons of black.'

119

'I shouldn't be telling you this now. You ought to be going home. I'm being selfish.'

'That's right. And I'm loving every minute of it. Have you considered reading it on the BBC? It surpasses any story at bedtime I've heard.'

'Do you listen to that?'

'Only as therapy, when I'm sick of stage management. I think, there but for the grace of God I might be intoning down a mike as a substitute for cocoa and Mogadon.'

'Or Radio One.'

'Or sex.'

'That's subversive.'

'Depends how you look at it. In overpopulated countries it's compulsory.'

'Sex?'

'No, you fat head; a "Book at Bedtime".'

Having begun her account it was impossible to abbreviate it, and by the time Olivia had finished the light from the street lamps had been replaced by a whitening sky.

'It's a really peculiar situation,' Judy agreed, 'and I think you've done very well to find out what you have. I want to think about it. I honestly can't be constructive till I've had some sleep. We need to weigh up all the things that people have said, try one story against another and see if there are any relations, whether any of the pieces fit. But a couple of things do strike me. One is that, being simply you, a member of the public and not the fuzz, you've been able to investigate only so far.

'Take what the neighbour said – and Raymond's interpretation may be close to the mark – you can't follow it up and go round searching for those men, to check. You've no way of testing the accuracy of anyone's statement nor can you insist on systematic recollection. You have to rely on accounts that may be riddled with private motives. That group in the pub might have felt guilty because they knew so little about Rita and they might have been over-compensating for that, or just happy to have a go at giving you help: for example, when she knocked over a glass it could have been the drink, not a strained wrist. You're subject to the whim of others and the level they are prepared to confide. You've been told that Mrs Dale is ashamed that Rita left home and assume that she's searching for her because, like Charles, she must still be alive. (It's a wonder you haven't had nightmares after Mrs Booth's unhinged confession; I shall have.) But after what she said to you, it seems to me that there's more to it than that. The woman's as mad as her mother. She's not just looking for Rita. She wants revenge. What was it she said?'

'In the end folk get their deserts.'

'Deserts for what, in this case?'

'I've no idea. Though, apparently, it isn't anything that I would ever do in spite of looking like her.'

'Rita's landlady?'

'That's right. Elizabeth Drew.'

Judy fluffed up the cushion at her elbow and replaced it with busy neatness. Then she switched off the light and walked to the window. 'There's the other thing that struck me, Olivia, only I'm not sure this is the right moment to discuss it. Neither of us can be objective after what we've seen tonight.' It was the first time she had admitted shock and, her body slack with fatigue, she leant her forehead against the glass as if controlling nausea.

'I'm sorry, Judy. I shouldn't have phoned.'

'Don't be stupid. If you hadn't I should have felt slighted.' She hesitated. 'Look, Olivia, I'm in no state to work this out and I don't want you to think that I'm deprecating your interest in Rita Dale, but I'm more concerned about something else. We shouldn't ignore the fact that ever since you started looking for her there have been offensive incidents of some kind or another focused upon you.'

121

'I've thought about that, but they are coincidences. On Monday night that bloke was abusive because Earl's black, and the barman's wife explained the man at the Gate – Josh.'

'Other people's reasons, Olivia. That doesn't make them right. I'm not convinced. It's a deception to argue coincidence. Too much has happened. In five days! You yourself are dissatisfied with Mrs Winterton's rationalization of the telephone calls – you confess to being convinced, intuitively, that they are meant for you – and then there's tonight. Olivia, I don't like it, but I have to go. This play can't get by without stage management; it's got little else.' But she did not laugh and, her face to the glass, she squinted up the well which was always in shadow. 'So I can't stay with you. That's why I want you to pack a case and come and doss down with me.'

Astonished, Olivia exclaimed fatuously, 'You're not serious?'

'I am.'

Turning, she presented her face. The skin was mottled, pocked by dilated pores, but not only through weariness; it was not only weariness that inflamed the eyes within puckering lids and dragged the expression. It was fear. And Olivia thought, I had no right to impose it; even friendship is not justified in exacting so much.

She said, 'No, Judy; you've done enough. There are limits.'

'You don't believe that. There aren't.'

'Oh, Judy.' It was hard to answer. 'Please don't be hurt; I'm not fobbing you off. But I can't accept. That would be running away.' She had argued coincidence; now she was admitting that was improbable but Judy did not rebuke.

'I've never been an admirer of gratuitous bravery. Stay at my place till things cool down.'

'I can't know when that will be.'

'Still, a few days away would be some respite.'

'Don't, Judy. I should be sorry, I know.'

'In that case . . .' She left the window. 'Now I must go.'

'You're exhausted. You mustn't drive back before you've had a nap. I feel shattered, and I had three hours' sleep upstairs.'

'I'll see how I feel after another cup of coffee.' Which Olivia made.

Having drunk, they sat in silence. Like two who had partaken in a vigil, their responses spent, they contemplated without vigour the emotions of the night and were blunt to the prod of dawn.

At last Olivia spoke. 'You have the bed.'

'I think there's a sleeping bag in the van. That'll do.'

'No. Don't argue. I've a sleeping bag somewhere.'

'OK. If I've gone before you wake, take as read my best of luck for the audition on Saturday.'

'Thanks. I meant to write but didn't have time. How did you know?'

'Alan told me.'

'So you're in contact again?'

'No. The telephone conversation when he told me about your audition was the death-rattle of a mouldering relationship.'

'And you didn't say! We've spent the whole night talking about me, about my affairs, and you kept quiet about this!' She was alert again, woken by shame. 'But you have to go to sleep.'

'I don't think I shall anyway. I'm done in, but through the sleep barrier. We finished, really, last week-end, but being Alan he had to have it in duplicate. I've known for weeks that it was inevitable, but I kept deceiving myself. I loved him. Truly; I did. Though there were things about him I couldn't take.'

'But they didn't matter. You said that he'd relax when he'd got work.'

'I'm not referring to his posing and egotism. What

123

stuck in my craw was his collector's mentality. He'd staple a reserve ticket on anything and he tried fixing one on me. I wouldn't have objected quite so decidedly had I been consulted; I'm not promiscuous. But when the ticket comes to be regarded as a receipt of purchase and no one else has permission to view the goods, then I'm for out. The imagery's deliberate; that's how he saw me though he called it "adoring" and "cherishing" – using words like that. So when he was thwarted, when he finally assimilated that his name wasn't the only one on the ticket, naturally it was my fault. There could be no other explanation.'

Olivia nodded. 'I can guess. He spoke to me on the phone on Tuesday.'

'God! It was awful. He was petulant at first: "You think more of Olivia." He couldn't understand why, if he were my feller, I could want to have friends. He wasn't only objecting to other men. In fact I think he could have pretended to tolerate them; it was the idea of close friendships with women that he found, incredibly, disgusting. By women, of course, he meant you. When I refused to be coerced he became vicious. Playing second fiddle on account of a woman wasn't his idea of a good time. His words.'

Above them in the street a milk-float rattled. Soon there would be the newspaper boy, the postman, the electrician next door revving up his van; all premature. The night had not yet ended.

'If that's how he thinks, Judy, you'll be pleased it's over, eventually.'

'I already am. I couldn't believe what I was hearing, and it all came so pat; almost as if he were reciting a part. He must have been storing it up for weeks. I didn't argue. I had no wish for a reconciliation and in any case I was too shattered by what had gone before. I had told him something, you see; something that happened a month or so ago. I had expected him to understand and

124

sympathize, though the expectation was really a need. His reaction was horrible: accusing, blaming me for what I had done. That started the row and he went on to you.'

Hunched in her chair, a finger smoothing a seam of her denims, she assembled the memories. Olivia waited.

'On Saturday evening as we came down here we were talking about that kerb crawler. I hope you haven't been bothered again?'

'No; that was the only time.' Before Judy's seamed face the lie was justified.

'I pointed out that we automatically assumed the person to be a man and you asked if I'd met any women kerb crawlers. Immediately after that we walked into here; I commented on it and your question was lost. I wanted to answer it but we had too many other things to talk about. Just before we watched the recording of "Mystery of the Week" I introduced the subject again but the moment wasn't appropriate, particularly for something so grim. Perhaps, had I confided in you, there would have been less urgency to tell Alan.'

'I'm sorry.'

'No. I'm not sorry. His attitude showed him up. I haven't met any women kerb crawlers, you see, Olivia, but I've been taken for one.'

Outside, a car slowed at the corner then accelerated. They flinched.

'I was driving the theatre van piled up with stuff and I passed a woman at a bus-stop. There was no shelter; it was bucketing down with rain and I knew that she had at least twenty minutes to wait. So I stopped and backed up. "Want a lift?" I shouted, leaning across and fiddling with the door, then inanely because she wasn't rushing to accept, "It'll be a squeeze but worth it." She put her hand to her stomach as if she were about to throw up and sidled behind the board displaying the timetable, and I was so astonished I just sat at the wheel, staring.

125

It was unbelievable. She was wearing a beige coat and the rain had soaked through, making a great rust-coloured stain across her shoulders and there was another across the top of her thighs. She had a plastic rain hat shaped like a sou'wester and water was running off the brim on to her face. She kept twitching her cheeks to flick it away and licking her top lip to stem the drops, but I suddenly realized that it wasn't rain on her face but tears. When I comprehended this I wanted to say something to her but I couldn't think of anything and then she said – whispered, really, but I read from her lips – "Please go away." '

'That's terrible.'

In the morning light Judy's face was colourless; a thin glitter snailed down a cheek.

'But you must have misinterpreted,' Olivia reasoned, stretching towards her. 'Probably she was distressed about something else and didn't want an observer.'

'No; it was me. And there was nothing I could say. I drove off.'

'It's appalling to be faced with that. And then having to go without correcting her.'

'It's more appalling if for some reason she expected it. I went because I was thinking of her.'

Olivia argued no more. They sat together reflecting while the morning sounds thickened and the room round them assumed the shape of day.

Then gently, removing the plimsolls speckled with paint and trying not to interrupt the oncoming sleep, Olivia eased her into bed and thanked her for what she had done.

'No probs,' she murmured. 'Felt I was back on the job. Because . . . funny thing . . . not like clearing up a room done over . . . more like a stage set. Weird.'

She had gone when Olivia woke, roused by the lunch-time scuttle of children. She had made the bed, just as she had tidied up the rest twelve hours earlier, obliterating all signs of the intruder's presence. But there was one sign she had been unable to remove though she had prevented its discovery in the brittle dawn hours. When Olivia rolled up her sleeping bag she flicked aside the cushion which Judy had so meticulously arranged. It tumbled over and lay like a small fat animal on its back, showing its belly. Out of which innards squeezed where a knife had plunged.

Picking up the cushion, pushing back the flocks and smoothing her fingers along the wound, she felt sweat spring as a point explored her own flesh and, seeing once again objects which revolved, writhed, twisted dizzily at the turn of a camera, Olivia watched their secret begin to uncoil, spread out and promise a comprehensible shape.

·

Chapter Nine

She was a long time before she found the fragment of paper, not in her handbag but in the pocket of her blouson where she had pushed it on Wednesday night. Upstairs, having dialled the number, she listened to the repeated signals and became apprehensive that her purpose would be frustrated by his not being there. His co-operation was essential.

'I hope you haven't been waiting long. I had the record player on rather loud,' he apologized. Though physically he had the same sex as Alan there was no other resemblance; they were at opposite ends of the continuum. On another occasion recognizing this she would have rejoiced but now she was merely thankful.

'Steve, have you still got that key of Rita's?' It was an unnecessary question but, not yet prepared for what she might find there, she could not request entrance outright.

'You mean you'd like to get in?' he said it for her. 'Certainly. No trouble. Have you had an idea?'

'I just thought it might be helpful to have a look,' she evaded. Then, sorry because he deserved more, 'I'm not suggesting that we may discover where she has gone, only that we may pick up hints about what happened.'

'That's possible. We may get a lead.' His answer was too prompt, to conceal disappointment, but the attempt was brief. 'It may be too much to hope we find a letter with a forwarding address,' and simulated a laugh.

'Yes. That would be too convenient.'

'When do you want to go? I'm free any time.'

On the point of replying, 'Immediately', she was halted by a flickering recollection, a duty already redundant but which she must perform. 'There's something I have to attend to.' She did not know how many hours to allow. 'Could you manage six?'

'Of course. Would you prefer to meet at the house or in town, say outside the station?'

'I'll see you at the house.' But her eyes on her goal, she sensed windows curtained against her and though it was summer there was ambushing darkness between the lamps, and she could not walk down that street alone. 'No, Steve, on second thoughts I'd rather not meet there. Let's make it outside the station.'

'Fine. Till six, then.'

'Thanks.'

She replaced the handset and stood puzzling over what she must do, but the telephone claimed her attention.

There was a gush of questions: 'How long's this been going on? Have you been receiving abusive calls? That operator made me feel as if I were first suspect,' and her explanations. Followed by: 'Your rail ticket arrived this morning. Rather than put it in the post since you might not receive it before you leave tomorrow, I gave it to Ray to drop in. He said he'd be passing. I'd hate to question his reliability but he was up to his eyes in Snow Cem at the time, metaphorically speaking. Is the ticket with you?'

The concern was irrelevant. Tomorrow was meaningless. The future was bounded by a room beyond Elizabeth Drew's door. Without bothering to check, she answered, 'It's here. Thanks for the trouble.'

'All part of the service. I must return to the monthly accounts. It's as well one of us isn't just a pretty face. Funny how at drama school they never said I'd need my O-level maths. Best of luck with the Piccolo. Do us proud, love.'

The draught was as chill as moonlight and walking to the door she examined the hole. Perhaps with cardboard and sellotape she could make a temporary repair. There was a precedent in a window upstairs, so this mimicked normality would prevent alarm when Mrs Winterton returned. Olivia wished the old woman to learn about the episode from her, calmly and simply, not from deduction.

Activity was a beneficial distraction. Looking round Mrs Winterton's kitchen she found an empty carton under the sink and, surprisingly, in a drawer a roll of sellotape mossy with fluff. From a newspaper under the telephone she cut out a rectangle, tailored it to the buckled lead and transferred the pattern to the side of the box. The next stage was laborious; cardboard admits a steel point less readily than does the fabric of a cushion and, when it had finally punctured it, the bread saw left whiskery serrations along the edge. She plucked and picked until it was smoother, prised open the lead flaps and slotted the piece in. It fitted so well there was no need for sellotape and she smiled, admiring her handiwork, pleased too because it suggested an advance, even a small victory. No one could see into the hall now; the spy-hole was shuttered.

Tidying up, she stroked flat the newspaper she had cut at and, looking out, framed in the space she had created, was Rita Dale's face. It was older than it had been on the television and did not scowl at the photographer but it was still private and unsmiling, the eyes pursed with distrust.

'I shan't hurt you,' Olivia told her. 'I'm not crazy. I shan't lock you out, or make you clean his boots, or womb you up.'

When she had thrown the hacked cardboard into the bin and returned the saw, she laid a page over Rita's face and folded the newspaper. Promising that she would read the report over lunch, she pretended that the postponement was not caused by what it might contain but by her next task.

'May I speak to the operator who intercepts our calls?' she asked and dictated the number.

'We all do, whoever's on shift.'

'Can you tell me anything about them?'

'What do you want to know?'

It was an unanswerable demand. Until she was offered some substance she had nothing on which to base questions. 'I thought you might have an idea . . .' She floundered.

'Would you like to speak to Customer Relations?'

'I don't think so, thanks.'

'Well, I can tell you that we don't make a report and we're not private dicks, so we don't ask the caller's name or trace the number. That's not possible, anyway.'

'I see.'

'There's been only one this morning since I came on at eight, and that seemed genuine.'

'Yes.' She could not bring herself to ask whether there had been calls on Wednesday evening or Thursday when the house had been empty for over twelve hours. All she knew was that none had got past the operator during the previous night. 'Do you think this . . . persecution . . . has stopped?'

'Your guess is as good as mine, but it could have. It often does after several days; the caller is frightened off.'

'That's what I understood; this has never happened to me before.' She recollected her mother's story, the mention that once the calls had been intercepted Gillian and her husband had been no more disturbed. By a disappointed woman formerly loved by Alex. And making the connection, Olivia thought, horrified, Could my tormentor be Alan? He would believe himself to have as much reason as did the one whom Gillian had succeeded. But he could not be responsible, she told herself, relieved; because Judy was with him on Saturday

131

night and most of Sunday. Even so, remembering his malevolence, she was visited by a new apprehension.

The operator was saying, her tone more sympathetic, 'It's not nice, I know, picking up the phone and hearing all the filth and sewage some of them pour out. We get it here from time to time, especially at night.'

'My caller doesn't speak.'

'One of those, is he? They're worse than the foul-mouthed brigade, in my opinion. If you're sharp enough you can answer back, give them some of their own medicine, but the silent ones give me the shakes. It's like he's got you on a string, playing cat and mouse. And, of course, if he can quote the subscriber's name when we ask, he's put through like everyone else. But obviously yours doesn't know your name, which is cheering.'

'Mine is not the name in the directory. But I'm certain he knows where I live.' Had he trailed her in his car, observed her through the bathroom's unscreened glass or, concealed by shadows, watched the throb of the house through the clear panes in the front door? 'When he had found the house, it would be relatively simple to trace the owner, then look up the telephone number in the book.'

'As far as I know, generally all they do is hit on a number, but you know the circumstances. Look, I shouldn't be doing this but there's a note Tony left when he went off shift. If I can find it. Right. It says, "Caller rang 756433 at twenty-two fifteen. Said we could lay off." The cheeky devil.'

A quarter past ten last night. While another was in her room? Or were caller and invader the same person who had concluded his evening with a message to the operator after he had finished his ravaging work? She shivered. 'Won't you be carrying on, then?'

'Because some unidentified pervert gives us per-mission to stop? Not on yours. It might well be a ruse —

132

you can't put anything past that type – and in any case the service is for a fortnight, free. If you'd like us to discontinue it you'll have to speak to the supervisor.'

'I'll tell Mrs Winterton. Thank you for being so helpful.'

'You're welcome. Bye.'

Encouraged by the operator's good sense, Olivia went down to the basement thinking, If it is a ruse it won't be successful. She said it wouldn't affect what she did. She will make sure he doesn't get through to me. And he won't try any other way. He will stay anonymous. He and his coward breed come by stealth: along a silent telephone wire, or with quiet engine stalking your back, or creeping furtively upon a deserted house. He and his kind do not come in the light.

Thus finally she conquered the fears which since waking she had striven to control; for as her eyes flinched at the sight of the cushion sliced by an unknown hand, her neck had pricked at the memory of a faceless threat behind a car wheel and her ears had listened again for the voiceless presence at the end of the wire. Now, more peaceful, she embraced the afternoon hours, looking neither at the night that had passed nor towards the one that jutted ahead; and with a sense of release she savoured each moment and what it brought.

She watched the slivers of cheese curl and pile into a soft drift against the grater; she examined the vegetables' convectional patterns in the pan of boiling soup; opening a bag of fruit, she gazed at the smudged stipple on the skin of a pear. Thoughts were shapeless; she let them glide by and did not attempt to give them form.

Later as she sat in the bath, her legs brown and skin taut, she received a stranger novelty. Usually she regarded with a mild disappointment some of her features, others with a guilty pride, but now they excited a childlike attention. Her soaping hands massaged the line of a thigh and the dip of breasts, explored the secret whorls of an ear, and found them all mysterious, the well-spring of awe. She did not seek to explain this, nor did she reason why, cocooned by a silk foam, her body became a pupa, a chrysalis, which she contemplated as a thing autonomous and detached from herself. For she was an actress, content to bide her time until the metamorphosis was complete.

So when she dressed in clean underwear, fetched the yellow sweat-shirt airing by the boiler and pulled that over a blouse, she did not question for what she was preparing. Unhurried, she was not flustered when at last she remembered that the appointment that had eluded her was at the police station, calculating that she had time for that before she met Steve. When, leaving the house, she found an envelope on the mat containing a ticket and a pencilled message, 'Sock it to them, love Raymond' she was indifferent and unaffected by nerves. And when she placed the envelope in her bag she was not startled to discover that, poking out of the usual litter, were the newspaper and the video cassette.

'You look pale,' Stephen greeted. 'Are you OK?'

'No less than I ever am. I had a late night.'

'It wasn't meant as a criticism. Only, it's very noticeable. You look bleached out.'

'No doubt there'll be a regeneration.'

He smiled. 'A straightforward revival will be enough.'

She did not argue.

They walked through the town. Stephen talking. 'I've been thinking a lot about Wednesday night. It was interesting that they all had something to say once they were invited to think. I had trouble getting their talk into some sort of order, trying to separate the wheat from the chaff, mainly because I couldn't be certain which was one and which was the other. It's a question of likelihood. I mean, the idea about murder was silly; obviously Mrs

Drew did nothing violent, but those fantasies were enough to remind you that someone else might.'

She did not remind him that someone had. Nor did she point out that there were kinds of violence other than physical assault. She remembered that there had been bags stacked on the pavement, securing departure, and in the kitchen behind the secretive 'best' room, the strike of a young girl's bayonet tongue; and, blenching, she saw a lawn on which were rucksack and boxes and heard her own voice shouting farewells above the idling of a theatre van.

'However, you have to keep in mind that some things they said may have no bearing on the situation at all,' Stephen continued. 'As Nick insisted, every little detail's not forced to be connected and I expect that story of Trudi's is one of them – how Rita went hysterical at her joke when she was helping with her zip. What you have to remember there, because it may be significant, is that Rita couldn't use her hand; the way she laughed then cried is unimportant. Yet that's the bit that nags. I can't get it out of my mind; it haunts me. It won't go away. It's as if it were trying to tell me something that I should pay attention to. But that's illogical.'

'I don't think so,' but she could go no further. As he spoke, she too was haunted; by a face. But it did not laugh, ironic, at a jokey remark. It shuddered, unable to receive an uncalculated generosity, its flesh bloated by tears under a film of rain. Tears which, later, Rita had shared.

'Some suggestions were outrageous, of course, such as Rita's stealing money. It's unfair to offer that as the reason for her suddenly having it because we can't imagine any other.'

She did not tell him that Raymond had suggested a bribe. Ahead of them she could see two gaps between the houses. The second, unblocked by television vehicles, was her street.

'You have to be careful that an idea doesn't become fixed, particularly when you can't prove it. I thought she was upset the night she got drunk, and so did Karen and Trudi, but we could easily be reading that into the situation to find a reason why she's disappeared. Really, her behaviour wasn't so different from normal. When Karen said she thought that Rita was trying to shut something off she was describing Rita, full stop. I ought to know.' He paused, dismayed by the bitterness. Defensive, he added, 'I mean, she never said anything to me about a strained wrist, though I saw her home. But you have to admit,' struggling to be just, 'that could be Karen's imagination; I doubt if she were in a state to remember what anyone said. However, her claim that Rita had a stepfather must be right.'

That had been the first time Stephen had learnt of him. Hearing his voice twang and the street now upon her, Olivia found his hand, glad of their reciprocal need. In this manner they walked together towards Elizabeth Drew's house.

They were in without fuss and there was no director, no woman with a clipboard, no young girl dashing to powder her face, but her stomach was snatched as it had been then, as it always was before walking on to a set. Though this was not a set; it was not built to create an illusion of reality; it was the hall of a small terrace-house, unassuming and plain. The first time she had entered she had leant against the door, panting after her flight from Alan's harsh face as he had asked her about Judy's next visit. Then, she had sensed a menace to something she treasured but could not identify. Now, again she felt panic; and, looking round this hall so similar to the one where she lived, she wished she had never left that other and that this evening and night would be a continuation of her own private day. Because, though there was no Alan waiting by the gate and this narrow space was empty of cables and camera, the hall still had the capacity to present a crisis. Today, however, this danger she felt was not confined to her own life; it embraced those that had existed inside this door. Folded within the yellow sweat-shirt and cotton trousers, the pupa stirred.

'That's Rita's room,' Stephen told her, pointing.

She delayed with: 'Shall we look upstairs first?' and saw his relief.

The stairs were uncarpeted, the treads covered with strips of linoleum nailed into place. Matting, its edges bound with plastic tape, led them along the landing and into the bathroom from which, as from Mrs Winterton's, could be seen the backs of houses along the parallel street. After this, the likeness ceased for the bath was modern and undistinguished, no cobwebs rigged the ceiling, no insects dried on the sill and there was no dust to skitter and roll in the draught. Nothing hinted a young girl's use or why it had ended. Not knowing for what they were searching, they pushed open the next door into the bedroom over the kitchen, small as Mrs Booth's but not a monument, simply a dump for discarded possessions; and though it had been sometime tenanted, it was not by a ghost. For in a space made between suitcases, cracked lampshades and vacuum cleaner without a bag, was a child's cot. Yellow flannelette was tucked round the mattress and a cellular blanket lay folded at one end. Starched and ironed, a linen picture book invited and a soft toy gazed through the bars, expectant.

'She hadn't any children,' Stephen remarked.

'Do you think this was . . . in hope?' After Charlie, anything was possible.

'No, I don't. I'm not writing that off,' he assured her hastily, 'but considering other evidence. What is called hard facts. I heard a baby once. Rita said it belonged to a guest.'

As they opened the next door, metal coat hangers

rattled on a hook, drawing to their attention the absence of wardrobe or cupboard for clothes. The only furniture was a bed, a chair, a dresser and a carry-cot resting on a tin trunk once an emblem of domestic service and in keeping with this room whose square of carpet was thin and faded and whose curtains hung in meagre folds. Attempts had been made to soften this austerity. A pot of ferns had been set on the dresser; a Van Gogh print, unframed, had been tacked to the wall; a misty demi-john holding a miniature garden had been placed in the hearth; and though the bed had no coverlet, it had been provided with deep rose blankets which looked friendly and warm.

Except for the addition of a small table, the second bedroom was a copy of the other even to the cot.

'She seems to have a lot of guests,' Olivia said. 'This place is a hotel.'

'More like a hostel. Still, who needs more than the basics when you visit? And it's all meticulously clean.'

They went downstairs. 'Now for it,' he said.

She could contrive no further excuse. Holding herself taut against the view she dreaded, she noticed that his hand shook as he turned the knob. But it was not as they had expected and, poised in the doorway, they heard the whistle of expired breath and felt the tension slip off.

'Someone's tidied up.' Then apologizing for the superfluous observation, 'I was ready for something else.'

'You can say that again.' She meant, say the first sentence again, because words made this normality permanent; they insisted that her vision of the room dissolving once more into chaos was a mirage.

'The television people must have done it.'

'That's unlikely. It could have been the owner. I gather it's the owner the police always inform when there's been a burglary – if the tenant's absent, I suppose.' She did not explain how she knew this for she had not told him about the previous night. Her account would have prompted his sympathy and returned her to yesterday's concerns; she did not want that. 'This house is rented from a Mr Catchpole – the neighbour told me. That must be why the police haven't searched for Rita. Or Mrs Drew. There was no need. They simply contacted Mr Catchpole; the neighbour said they had brought him round. Presumably he allowed the television company in and then cleaned up later. That was thoughtful.'

'Yes. It must have been an unpleasant job. I wouldn't have liked doing it. I'd have hated folding things up, putting them back in the drawers.'

'Perhaps his wife helped him. Notice that we're assuming that the owner is male! She may be a woman.'

'Would that make this easier?'

'Probably not.' She thought of Judy. 'But a woman is more accustomed to intimate ministerings. In families it's generally she who nurses the sick.'

'Which must be rotten if by nature you're squeamish. This one couldn't decide where all Rita's stuff went, though. She's left a few things out.'

A pair of striped ankle socks lay knotted in a corner; a record sleeve was propped against a leg of a chair, the record still on the turntable. In the hearth stood a box full of a jumble of make-up, curling rollers, transistor batteries, a hoard of ringed beer mats, a Snoopy outfit and two felt-tipped pens.

'She may have left them like this on purpose, I suppose, to give the place a more natural look, so that it appeared that no one had ever disturbed it,' he suggested.

'And does it look natural – normal?' The evidence made the question unnecessary but to inquire had become a habit.

He laughed. 'Heavens, no! Rita couldn't keep a room like this. It was always a tip. In fact when I think about

139

it, the person who broke in must have had most of his work done for him. I'm sorry. That's facetious, a reaction after what might have been.'

She nodded. 'Her grandmother would agree.'

'And I shouldn't criticize,' he went on, contrite. 'I'm not that tidy myself. She might have kept her things better most of the time and I saw them at their worst. I didn't come often and didn't stay long. I was merely picking her up before we went out. I've thought about that. I was never in for more than a few minutes and I'm not a great observer, so that must be why I was confused by the programme. When I felt that the room didn't seem right it must have been that I'd never looked at it properly, never examined it closely. My visual memory must be poor.'

'It may not be a fault of your memory at all but the camera angles. Seeing an area from a different viewpoint you can often not recognize what is really familiar.'

'I expect you're right,' he answered, but he was not wholly convinced.

They stood together in the middle of the room, their eyes passing over the stacked magazines, the market stall ornaments, the plimsolls scabby with mud, the fat cushion whose holed fur had been hidden against the duvet by a considerate hand.

'I'm pleased that someone has put her things away, that they haven't been left out, even though there was no one to see. Like corpses after an attack. But it doesn't help us to find her,' he mourned, dejected.

'No.' She did not tell him that the frustration did not matter now, that it was hardly more than a disappointment to be got through until a movement at the edge of her mind took a precise form.

'We oughtn't to be here. It's her place.'

Acquiescent, she turned to follow him and saw paper lift and skitter across the chest of drawers as he passed.

140

She stopped its fall but before she had pinned it securely under a magazine she had seen the logo and name.

'Do you ever visit the pawnbroker, Steve?'

'Come off it. What have I got to pawn?'

And what had Rita? They had come to examine a dismantled room and to look for clues that might lead them to its tenant; now that it was set to rights and again private, it accused them of intrusion.

'There's a pawn ticket here.'

'That's her business,' he disapproved.

But for the moment her condition of the past week and its preoccupation were reasserted and though guilty at the prying, she lifted the receipt. Aloud, propitiating forgiveness, she read: 'One hunter watch, gold . . . £42; one cigarette case, silver . . . £3; one pair of plus-fours, 33" leg . . . £1; one leather belt with ornate buckle . . . £1; one lace christening robe . . . £2; one white shawl . . . £1.'

There was a long silence.

At last, 'I wish you hadn't read that.'

'So do I, now.'

'It explains the night in the pub, but she didn't spend all that amounts to, thank God. Poor girl, she must have been desperate to pawn all that. She was ripped off, too. Three pounds for a silver cigarette case!'

'No; its only value is the weight of the metal. We had a neighbour once who ran a jeweller's shop and gave loans on the side. He would have been interested only in the watch. I imagine that this fellow was, too, but since she left it, he must have agreed to take the case and clothes as a personal favour. He certainly would have no outlet for the clothes.'

'They weren't worth pawning.'

'She wasn't concerned with their value,' Olivia murmured.

You tell her it's the last thing I'd have imagined coming from her, she had said; but it was not her granddaughter's conduct that had aged her. It was the despoiling of the spirit who had kept her young, forever reaching towards the reunion with one who had been granted the fairy touch and who would dazzle her confined life with joy.

'How do you mean, not concerned with their value? She bothered to pawn them.'

'She may not have intended to. They may have been the result of an impulse.' She hoped they were.

'I don't see why. She must have thought carefully about what she was doing. It's a strange collection. Plus-fours! However did she come to possess a pair of those?'

'It would be the watch she went for. After that, the choice would be random.' Opening the trunk, grabbing, squeezing the plunder into her bag, fearful lest at any moment she would hear the key in the lock, the steps ascending the stairs.

'Went for?' she heard Stephen say and then, 'I see.'

She looked across at him and comprehended the disillusionment in his face. 'I assumed you understood, Steve,' she apologized.

'Where from?' he asked bleakly.

'Her grandmother. They belonged to her great-uncle who was killed in the last war.'

'That's obscene.'

She could think of nothing to console him except: 'No doubt she means to recover them as soon as she can.'

'That makes no difference.' He was picking at the door jamb like a child who pretends an intense absorption in order to appear unaffected by punishment. 'I said to you that one has to be careful that an idea doesn't become fixed. Talk about, physician heal thyself! I was totally blinkered; I automatically rejected Wayne's suggestion. He had nothing to base it on, of course. That is, as far as I know. Because, really I don't know her any better than he does. I can see that now. Olivia, I didn't know her at all.'

142

'I think that's how she wanted it.'

'Yes.' He moved into the passage. 'Do you mind if we go?'

'All right.' To extenuate their flight she said as she joined him, 'I expect we've seen everything of interest. This back room must be Mrs Drew's?'

'It's the sitting-room. She lived downstairs,' nodding towards the door at the head of the cellar.

'*Lived?*' She recalled the spartan bedrooms blank of a permanent occupier and their deduction that these rooms were intended for guests. She had forgotten Elizabeth Drew, had not wondered where she slept. 'She has made the basement into a sort of bed-sit?'

Indifferent, he answered, 'I suppose she must have. She was always down there when Rita shouted to say she was going out. She never left without doing that. She insisted, though she wasn't obliged. She was the lodger and looking after herself; she didn't have to keep her landlady informed.'

This is the house, Olivia recited to herself; this is the hall; her room is at the bottom of a flight of stone steps. Her arms were heavy; legs were cumbersome; the mind echoed with the rustle of a pupa that stretched.

'You go,' her voice said. 'I haven't finished. There's something I must see. No, please; you've had enough. Please don't wait. I'll give you a ring. You've been splendid,' and she watched fingers touch his cheek and felt it dimple under lips.

There was a handrail fixed to the wall and she used it to guide herself. It was thick and rigid and held her as she lurched. At the bottom, the window showed stalks of dandelions whose seed clocks dispersing whiskered the panes and freckled the light. More was not needed. On the other side of the door her eyes were not stopped by the shadows lying in bars nor did they blink at the stab of what they found. Because she had looked on it before, though she had not guessed its riddle. Now this

143

room would surrender it. For she was almost ready; it would soon be completed. The spun filaments were unfurling to release a new creature, delicate yet sure.

But first she must repair this ruin. She pulled off the yellow sweat-shirt, rolled up the sleeves of her blouse. And the only surprise she felt as she began on her task was that she had been so obtuse. She believed she had achieved detachment, for the cycle of hours of the one she had looked for had not taken over her own; but softly, imperceptibly, another had filled the place. Without her knowledge, she had been led by this other, and she had connived with her selflessness. Olivia now knew that it was the wrong woman whom she had sought.

Chapter Ten

Diligent as the policeman, she first examined the window and found, ghostly under the grey dusting powder, the scores of a chisel round the latch. Two nails had been driven through the frame to keep the sash immovable but that was the limit of the owner's concern. He did not conform to the generous person they had made him to explain Rita's unsmashed room. With the window secure behind her, she began on the drawers.

The task was as uncongenial as Stephen had imagined but she performed it conscientiously and without haste, keeping her hands steady and swallowing down the tart sickness as she folded the ripped underwear, stroked up the crunched jewellery into an envelope, threw away flattened tampons and replaced in its splintered box a twisted and split Dutch cap. And gradually her occupation was no longer a task but an unqualified service, a ceremony of healing. Each piece was taken up, smoothed into wholeness, cherished, found a place, as she did for the absent woman what Judy had done for her.

When she had finished the twilight had piled dense in the corners but a street lamp umbered its centre to translucent brown. In which light she prepared herself for a discovery that, after talking with the casting assistant, she had planned but shunned, and she could not control her revulsion as she took the cassette from her bag. The last time it was used had been by the one who entered Mrs Winterton's basement, by the one who had left it switched on, who playing it over had checked that the devastation he was engaged upon corresponded with this on the film, with the devastation she had just repaired. Contriving a scene that had puzzled Judy: like a stage set.

Olivia inserted the cassette and while it wound back she looked at the room she had re-created. The room that belonged to Elizabeth Drew. Though she could not assess that everything was positioned correctly, she was satisfied. Kicked furniture had been polished; earth spilt from overturned plants had been swept up and patted round the roots; the lanced cushion had been dressed with sticky tape. It was appropriate, waiting. Knowing that the cocoon's silk was ready to give up a pupa transformed. So, with a fearful exhilaration that screwed the muscles of her stomach, she saw as she bent to start the film, a moth twirl through the lamp beam and come to rest on the bright screen.

A street of stone terrace-houses was slotted into the frame and one grew larger, pushing out the street. Her eyes were taken up the path and invited to peer into the cellar well which held the window behind her, then they were brought to a woman who came out of the door, closed it and ran to the gate. Watching critically, she thought, They did well to find an actress so like me, but surely I don't go around banging gates. Immediately there was a cut to a Telecom engineer's raised head, then herself hurrying away. Like someone whose mission was over; who had undertaken a job, done it competently then left. 'But it didn't stop there,' she murmured and rose to run the tape back to the scene the other had watched.

She looked at Rita's face with interest, younger in this photograph but no less guarded than the one she knew, and she followed the objects of her room as they were spun by the camera's lash; but reconstructed violence no longer disturbed her. Instead, she was shocked by the presenter's words. They linked the 'scene you have

146

just witnessed' with Rita and implied that it was her room that had been shown. Agitated, she jumped from her chair, stopped the cassette and rushed upstairs, panic-stricken lest the girl's room, too, had been attacked, jostled by the necessity to put it right, compelled by the instinct to protect as urgent as it had been when she first made the girl's acquaintance and which had grown more insistent during the last few days.

Inside the door she stood panting, feeling foolish, irritated at being so easily misled. For anyone who knew the rooms could distinguish this from the one in the television programme. There, the ceiling was low, the light stooped in cautiously from the garden above; here, deep cornices raised the height of the walls and a bay window greeted the sun. She would have enjoyed living in it herself and, switching on the light, she surveyed what she had surrendered: the bed, wider than her own; the chest of drawers she had placed there instead of the cheap cupboard downstairs; the wardrobe more grand than her jumble sale tallboy; the armchair more luxurious than her dilapidated sofa empty of springs. Collected from second-hand shops or dumped by more affluent friends, this furniture was not expensive, neither was it particularly tasteful, but it was the best in the house and from it a stranger would deduce that this was her room. There was little wonder that the basement had been thought, by landlord, police, television people, to house her lodger. She had made the choice deliberately, giving Rita the less shabby, spoiling the girl to compensate for a relinquished home. From whose obsessive neatness she generally rebelled but on this occasion she had adopted her mother's example of sedulous cleaning. Had in one respect gone further, she thought, her mind shying away from the knowledge of what Rita had done, and to calm it with order she removed the record from the turntable, patted it into the sleeve and flicked out a screw of paper trapped down the chair's arm. Straightening the creases, she saw that it was a rough draft of the girl's letter whose copy she had read some weeks before, that had been in an envelope together with the two bent fragments that just now she had tried to forget. Again, to shut off that memory, she sought distraction and feeling her way to the basement, she returned to the programme on the cassette.

After, diminished by distance, she had been lost at the end of the street, the camera switched again to a Telecom engineer who walked round the van to his mate and lit a cigarette. He took a puff, spoke to the other, then the camera moved back to the house, over which shot came sentences she had not heard before: 'Did you see that, Dave? She was leaving in a hurry. Makes you wonder what's been going on. Looks black for somebody.' There was a slight pause as the 'Pennine News' credits came up and music began, but through this came clearly though fragmented, further words: 'I wouldn't mind if one I knew shifted as quick . . . but when a couple of women get together, there's no room for a man . . . playing second fiddle on account of a woman isn't my idea of a good time.'

For a few seconds the words hung slack in the air, then they twanged taut and she was off the settee, kneeling in front of the set, playing the scene over and over again, trying to distort the speech to an acceptable shape, to impose an innocent meaning, to make it conform to her disbelief. But she could not and finally she depressed the button and crawled into the diluted light under the window, away from the darkness of the set. She had heard from someone that the actor had been asked to improvise. In such a programme that was inexcusable. He should not have been invited to comment on the way she had left, suggesting that some heated quarrel had caused the haste which the Telecom engineer claimed to have seen. But that was less important than the effect of his last words. Someone had told her that it had not been intended to keep his remarks in the programme, had confessed that they ought not to have gone out, but apology was useless. Because, she recalled, he had been asked to give the reaction of the 'ordinary man in the street'. Did this represent the view of the ordinary man in the street? For this actor, assured that most of his audience would approve, had expressed his resentment against any woman who might share the affection of the one he wished to possess. There on the screen she had been associated with a competition for affection; she had been accused as if personally she had come between this man and his girl, and she felt bruised and swollen by the punch of his spite.

Some of his words seemed familiar; his statement that playing second fiddle on account of a woman wasn't his idea of a good time, she thought she had heard somewhere before, and it sounded not impromptu but studied, almost as if he were reciting a part.

She wondered how other people would react to them but comforted herself that their effect would be transient and would be quickly absorbed beneath the wash of other sensations. They could influence few in their attitude to her. Then a memory shivered; she made a connection and again she was up, had switched on the light and was hunting for a handbag, was tipping out its contents and salvaging a newspaper she had seen when she had removed the cassette.

Once more Rita's face regarded her, this time out of a snipped frame, and thinking that this might block out other details in the picture, she was visited by the hope that when she lifted it something of the girl's closed nature would be uncovered – a passion, a recreation, even a pet – but there was nothing. The other still eluded her.

Speculation on the disappearance of seventeen-year-old Rita continued over the weekend as no more news came in, she read.

After nights without sleep, Rita's parents were in a state of collapse as they spoke to our reporter in their house in Cattlegate which was unusually quiet this Monday morning.

'She seems to have vanished off the face of the earth,' said Mr Dale her father, a shop manager. 'It is terrible for parents at a time like this when you don't know what has happened. I wish anyone who knows anything at all would speak up.'

They are particularly anxious to contact a Mrs Elizabeth Drew who Rita was living with at the time of her disappearance. As shown on Saturday night's Pennine News' 'Mystery of the Week' which first uncovered the incident, Drew, who is believed to be separated from her husband, was seen leaving her home in Hackney Street in a great hurry two weeks ago according to a Telecom employee working in the area.

'Her room being turned upside down in that way makes you think there had been some foul play,' Mrs Dale agreed, and violence has not been ruled out. 'I can't understand why this woman hasn't come forward,' she added.

It is several months since the brunette Rita went to live with Drew but Mrs Dale could not confirm whether there had been the normal rent-paying arrangement. However, she confirmed that Rita Dale was an impressionable young girl.

'We're staying by that telephone night and day till we hear something,' Mr Dale said. 'We're both worried stiff.'

It was the usual worthless report and her impulse was to stamp it into the waste-paper basket and apply a match but, arrested by the extravagance of her disgust, she read it again. The effect of 'Mystery of the Week' had lasted longer than she had predicted, she admitted to herself. The journalist had relied on it and gone much further than the programme's 'It is thought that the scene you have just witnessed may be connected with Rita's disappearance.' He had linked it with herself. Naturally he had not done this outright; the hint was sly. But by stating that she had left 'in a great hurry', then by mentioning in the next sentence the possibility of foul play and following that with a reference to her continued absence, he had led readers to a comfortable assurance of her guilt. 'There must be something in it,' someone had said.

That was not all. Examining the passage a second time and interpreting it out of feelings made raw by the workman's words, she identified that 'something'. For the strange interest in rent-paying arrangements was not as casual as it seemed; it was calculated to raise the suspicion that the lodgings she had provided might have been free as a result of some kind of intimate relationship: 'when a couple of women get together'. Which Rita had succumbed to, because she was young and 'impressionable'. The journalist made the arrangement a certainty with that insidious word.

She put aside the newspaper and for many minutes she sat, her hands gripped in her lap, while she waited for her pulse to quieten. It was not the insinuation itself that rocked her; love has many forms of expression and is not to be judged by outsiders' rules. What appalled her was the prurience fingering greasily a relationship that was private and delicate and offering it to the coarse public gaze. Infected by jealousy, the actor who was the Telecom man had played his part better than he had imagined. His words had been picked up by the journalist who had therefore added lechery to the suggestion of foul play. Though less conspicuously sensational, the report followed the style of many newspapers and endorsed their reputation. It was a small, cunning essay on their main ingredients: violence and sex.

She hoped that Rita had not seen it, though she did not think she would have noticed all that was there. Whatever her talents might be, they were not literary. Pulling the crumpled sheet from her pocket, she considered it again. The corrections made it harder to decipher than the neat copy but if she were to fetch that she could not avoid seeing what had been placed with it in the envelope. So she read this first attempt, saddened that Rita had felt she must copy it out, an action

151

which showed once again how defensive she was, and without trust. However, she winced at the 'Dear Mrs Drew', Rita's spontaneous address; the 'Dear Elizabeth' in the transcript had been a second thought.

Dad came after you went to the shops and I said I'd go with him. I know you have your~~e~~ own opinion, but I do'nt mind him and Il'l say not to come after, I'ave had enough with Mum. You ~~was~~ ~~were saying~~ said we would be better of fliting at the present, so ~~its~~ its' alright going with my Dad. He says I can stop if I like his hous and his ~~wife/s~~ wifes name is Phylis.

I saw Steve the night after that man had pushed himself across the step and I gave him the key like you said. I didn't tell him it was to keep an eye on the house. I did'n't see why he was being brought into it. I expect it'll stop again. You said it has stopped before for a bit when you ~~are'nt~~ ar'not at home.

I have not been to tell Mrs, Bellamy like you asked what with Dad coming first of and wanting to go as soon as I have packed. He saies I'm to write this while he gose to the garage to fill up and nip in to see a mate.

You can have my room back if that is convenient. I don't want the things I have left because my Dad says his going to buy me a lot of new. So good-bye now, with thanks.

Yours Faithfully,
Rita C. Dale.

It was not a letter to return to. There was nothing in it to muse upon or enjoy and she folded it quickly, wondering whether Rita would have said more than, 'So good-bye now, with thanks,' if she could have scraped together the words; then told herself firmly, no. In any case, more would have exceeded their agreement. Within her own terms the girl had been a considerate lodger; for example, she had always let her know when she was going out, which forestalled worries. That was her way of expressing appreciation and it had to suffice. When she had taken Rita on she had not wanted thanks or the obliged gratitude of a dependant. She had done it because, seeing the girl, she had felt driven.

About to replace the letter in her pocket, she saw on the reverse side a postscript which Rita had not transferred to the neat copy. Perhaps that had been prevented by her father's return. Even so, the haste to be gone which this betrayed was painful.

PS. Do/n't you worry about my wrist. Its nearly better but you should'nt have let that man get of so easily pushing in and then carrying on and shouting all that about me and you. I dont care what he saies about your visitors, he can say what he likes about them but not about me/ and you. Your not to think I ~~mindded~~ those women com/ing, they ~~didn't d'not~~ did not bother me much and I'm going with my Dad because I want and not ~~throw~~ thorough them or those men. I never said but I think it was those wommens' fault, they only got what they could expect because if they had put there foot down they would/n't have had the trouble.

Yes, she had felt driven. Rita's appearance, so withdrawn and vulnerable, had urged her predisposition to shelter. It was the strongest emotion she had. Shuddering, remembering what lay in the envelope, she admitted how deceived she had been.

The letter had done one small service; it had reminded her of the others and since she was here, she would go upstairs and check. She never knew when they might come. Sometimes she thought her house was like a hotel; no, more like a hostel, she corrected and smiled.

She smiled at the rooms, too. They were always ready and though she could not afford to furnish them more comfortably they were peaceful. That was all that was required. They provided a brief rest. She noticed that the leaves of a fern were brittle and she took the pot into the bathroom and watered it under the tap. She had been away longer than she realized; she could not remember how long. The occasions of flight merged. She had once told Mrs Bellamy – or it might have been one of the others – that she herself was lucky; she could get right away. But when ructions came, they hadn't a chance;

153

they could go no distance nor manage a permanent change. Economics and fear tied them. They could dare only a few days. They could seek no other protection for if they reported it, were seen anywhere near the police station, they would be punished before anything could be done. Last time after Mrs Bellamy had been here – or it might have been one of the others – he had struck so hard at her feeble threat of Authority that he had broken her spectacles. So now she avoided policemen; she could not risk his thinking she had been talking to one. She had been safe up here, though, and so were the others. That was why she put them upstairs. They were out of reach when the knocking started. She wondered what the neighbours made of it; and hadn't someone once suggested that it was her own husband knocking, coming to challenge a man who had replaced him? She wished it were as simple as that. But so far she had succeeded in dealing with it, except the night when Rita had let one in. She felt guilty about that because she had been hurt. Until then she had prevented the girl's being involved and hoped it was not the reason why, later, she had come home drunk.

She was growing tired; the day was nearly over but before she left she would find herself something to eat.

The shelves in the kitchen were divided into sections marked by sticky labels. Printed on these in the girl's handwriting were their names: Elizabeth and Rita. This precaution could appear to indicate scrupulous house-keeping but in fact was a separation typical of the girl. To share would have compromised her position as lodger and might lead to friendship. Rita didn't want that. So she had resented being included in the man's accusations, not caring, of course, whether or not they were accurate about the other women but insisting in her letter only that he should have been corrected about Elizabeth's relationship with herself. After that, it must have been a shock to hear her friend's joke as she helped with the zip — someone had told her that the girl had been practically hysterical. Sadly she wondered whether Rita's tears were a terrible private regret that she could not behave more naturally.

But, looking at the labels which emphasized the division of food that she herself had shopped for, she felt the rebuff and was stung by its unkindness. In defiance she took a packet of cream crackers from Rita's shelf, spread three biscuits with margarine, added slices of cheese and took them on a plate down to her room.

Sitting beside the television, its screen now blank of images, she was able to reflect more calmly on the effect of a few improvised words. Which had provoked false conjectures about her and had planted inaccurate deductions concerning her private life which distorted her generosity. But perhaps it was not so surprising. Delusion occurred without the prompting of any device. A man could approach another on a station believing that he had been the boy with whom he had played in his street. Thinking of this, she saw the moth glide to the lamp and heard its wings tapping inside the shade. Soon, satiated with light, it would fold and rest. And suddenly she felt anxious, not for herself but for the one who had taken her place. She was weary, but she must last a short time longer; there were things that must be said before she went away.

'I couldn't know that they would try to reconstruct it,' she apologized, 'or that you would play my part. Would you have done so had you suspected what might come of it? Had imagined that a young man's jealousy would swell the hatred beyond the screen's frame? For it already fermented. I have been abused, struck, up there in the hall. This would increase, rush to a climax, and I would go away. The break-in was a climax; it was a warning. I didn't clear up; I couldn't; I walked out of the

155

house immediately; I didn't even cancel the milk. I was free to go because Rita had done so already; she was out of danger. She had written her letter.

'But going, I left them with you. You who resemble me in features and have, like me, this urge to protect. Though you thought it was Rita you were protecting when in fact you had offered yourself as a substitute for me. An understudy, you would say, required suddenly to step under the lights. And so they transferred their attention to an actress. Because many would make no distinction; I do not have to remind you that people often cannot distinguish between actors and the characters they portray. If those who harassed you had stopped to think, they would have remembered that I was reported to have gone away, but I doubt if that knowledge would have deterred them. Even those who may have sensed that it was not I they pursued would find you an equally satisfactory prey, because you were implicated, having represented me on the programme. So they applied to you everything that had been hinted about me.

'For the men who harassed were not necessarily all like Josh who had a personal grudge and believed he was speaking to me when he said that he wasn't "standing for any more". (A man loses his self-respect when he can't keep hold of his wife.) No. That piece of film and the report in the newspaper gave licence to men besides those who had reason to seek revenge.

'There was an occasion in a hamburger restaurant when a man accosted you. He could have been one of those who knock, the one who telephones, a kerb crawler or a man innocent of such abuse, just eating a meal by himself; but surely he had read the report. Incited by that, he attacked you not because of your young man's colour, as was suggested, but because of his homosexuality. The deduction is feasible. You almost guessed this yourself when your friend Raymond apologized for his previous attitude to men like Earl, for Raymond's words "doing what they do" echoed the ferocious challenge of the man in Greasy Len's.'

She paused. 'I know this grieves you. I understand why you are ashamed. For you once confessed to Judy that you could not rid yourself of disgust when you thought of Earl with men, and now you ask yourself whether that is any different from Alan's revulsion for you. But your response to Earl's sexuality does not prove that you are no better than Alan or the man in the hamburger restaurant. You do not share their blame because you do not allow your feelings to alter your behaviour. You must not be so severe with yourself. It is hard to be entirely free of prejudices. They will leap up without our volition, but you have discovered what it is like to be the victim of one this week.

'There may be others, too, who would like to insult you. Mrs Dale is jealous of me; at least, I'm sure she must be because she thinks I have taken Rita from her. Miserable at her daughter's leaving home, she was gratified to be offered a culprit for her loss, particularly if that culprit were presented as disreputable, inferior to herself. Thus she was shocked by the journalist's description of me as "that type" but she did not object to it as did her mother. The old lady told you that Mrs Dale had allowed the man to put ideas into her head and words into her mouth. Since it was less humiliating to believe that someone had influenced Rita to leave her, she quickly adopted his suggestion that the girl was impressionable, though you remember that she was still testing the novelty of his word on her tongue.

157

'After this, the stepfather was clever enough to anticipate how the interview might be reported, and feared that this might recoil on you. Inviting you to visit them he tried to warn you – you mentioned to Earl that you thought he was holding something back – but finally he hadn't the courage. Then that morning in the market you rejected Mrs Booth's attempt to enlighten you.

'You have told me that the mother hoped I'd get my deserts. Well, she may be satisfied if she ever learns that others have taken their revenge.'

Her energy had almost gone. She was played out. But something remained which their minds cringed from and they had pushed it away, telling themselves that it was not their concern; they were not its target. It was meant for two others. That argument was an evasion, however. If they looked upon the thing together its horror might be exorcized.

So they watched as one lifted the envelope which had also contained the copied letter and neither turned away her eyes when the two bruised fragments fluttered out. Each had an edge which was uneven, chopped by blunt scissors that had cut through a word written by a ballpoint pen. She slid the two pieces together and read out: 'Dead' and the date which was the same as the one at the head of the letter. Then they watched as the pieces were turned over. The face had once smiled but now, sliced through, its halves had the rictus of a skull; hacked off, a leg hung from the bumper of an Army truck; the word scored into the back had raised weals across the broad khaki chest. Before the blades had gone through, the picture had been cancelled with deep lines connecting the opposite corners.

Together they stared. The young woman who had committed this act had lodged with one of them; she had been searched for by the other and occupied her thoughts; and each reflected as Stephen had done that she was still a stranger.

The remains of the photograph had been laid on the floor. Once it had been whole, lovingly treasured in an album or put out 'to air'; and faded, it had a dark border where light had been stopped by a frame. Now dismembered, cloven, his laughter sheared, the soldier looked up at them, his eyes still unclosed, and a ceremony seemed necessary. She bent down and gently, keeping the two pieces together, she revolved them until the harsh diagonal strokes took the shape of a cross.

Now it was over. She could go. She found her handbag, rolled down the sleeves of her blouse and pulled on the yellow sweat-shirt. Then she turned off the light. Upstairs she found that in all the rooms the lamps were on and rebuking herself for such absent-mindedness she switched them out. No curtains had been drawn; the house must have been like a beacon, but tonight it had fetched no one. Olivia smiled to herself. It was as it had been before.

Leaving the bedrooms she thought of Elizabeth preparing them for the others; she thought, too, of Judy restoring her own shattered place and was content that the one below, here in the basement, was again tranquil. So, reaching the hall, standing by the door as she had done that day of the filming, she did not experience apprehension and dread. Because she now knew that it was generosity and affection for which she had trembled, and that they were less fragile than she had feared. They had not cracked under the club of violence and abuse.

She went through the door and closed it carefully behind her, making sure that the catch slipped into place. She walked down the short path and passed through the gate. This time she was not moving to a director's instructions. This time she was free; herself.

159

She had finished the job, had completed what she had set out to do. But it wasn't like coming out of the theatre after you have given a good performance, when you are high. This was not elation she felt but sadness. It wasn't as you feel after a good performance when the energy is still pumping and you know it will continue for hours. It wasn't at all like coming off stage. Because she felt so tired and completely used up; her lent life had been ephemeral and now her body was a husk and she must wait for that which had gone from her to be replaced.

So it was some time before Olivia heard the footsteps behind her. At first, absorbed in this private renewal, she took no notice, expecting them to pass. But they remained and gradually she acknowledged that she was being followed. In front of her the street was empty and neutral, holed by darkness between the infrequent lamps; behind her, matched to her strides, was this threat. For a moment she considered rushing up a path, banging on a door and shouting for admittance, but she could not do it. Even had there been lights in a house, that might not have been possible, and to fetch someone from bed, noisily importuning assistance and thrusting her crisis into this sleeping normality, was beyond her. She had no idea of the hour.

She walked more quickly but the distance between them lengthened for only a minute; the steps jerked rapidly before becoming even again as they adapted to her speed. Then there was a slight catch in the rhythm and suddenly they were walking in unison, their legs swinging to the same beat, and there were no longer two patterns of echoes but one, fixed, undeviating, relentless; the pursuer concealed by the sound of the pursued. At which, sweat gathered and breath was erratic. Passing through the arc of a street lamp she cried out as a squat shadow edged under her; it grew and she saw it was her own. No other came alongside it, a measure of the space left her which she must preserve. But the light weakened and her frail tape was sucked into the night which reared before the next faraway lamp.

Then she was running and the feet behind her were not in time with hers now, they drummed out a new pace and she must not be overtaken by them and what they brought: a hydra head, one face masked by the windscreen of a car; one featureless and mute at the end of a phone; one thrust over a table spitting grease; one driven into her cheek turned from the smell of drink; one hissing venom; one fat with salacious gossip; one above the dungarees of a workman releasing hate. She must keep ahead of them but she was tiring, her body was old, its spirit had not yet returned. If she could reach the next lamp she would stop and face this thing that hunted her but it was closer, drilling her ears with obscenities and abuse, strident, without a pause.

Until at the thin edge of the light its ferocity slackened and her hearing became tuned to cadences, plaintive, which told her of those who sit lonely amid others' laughter, of men whose language is fists humiliated by jeers at the empty house, of those so unsure they dread inclusive affection, of all the desperate unloved whose caress is the fear they have dialled. But as together, prey and predator, they reached the light's core, these wraiths dissolved into breaths which sobbed pleas for her charity, which choked on the vista of paced streets empty of a figure yearned for, which surrendered all claims if only she would give assurance of life; while a hand reached out, touched her shoulder gently, pleadingly, and a name was called, the one she had recently shared.

And swinging round, Olivia saw, covered with tears so heavy that they could have been taken for rain, the face of Charlotte Dale.

Chapter Eleven

'How did you fare with the audition?' Mrs Winterton greeted. 'On Friday I was home and in bed before you came in and you were out again before I descended for breakfast yesterday, so I couldn't wish you luck. Last night I'm afraid I was the one keeping late hours. Well, tell me; don't hold me in theatrical suspense.'

Olivia grinned. 'You're doing that yourself. I don't know whether they want me, of course. They decide next week. But the audition went quite well, though it was one of those exploratory affairs when they give only half an ear to your prepared pieces because they're more interested to discover how you would fit their style – hence the assistant director leaps up and you're asked to improvise with him.'

'Really? What was the task?'

'My behaviour when pestered by a chap on a station. I had to push him on to the line eventually. The play they are opening the season with is *Masterpieces*.'

'I don't know it. I confess that the theatre stops for me with George Bernard Shaw.'

'There's been quite a lot written since then.'

'So I understand. Did you acquit yourself well?'

'As a matter of fact I was rather pleased with what I managed.'

'That's splendid. Perhaps the events of the past week have borne fruit. Yes, I mean that precisely.' She paused; her eyes held Olivia's. 'This morning I had a long telephone conversation with your charming friend, Judy. It seems that I have not been supervising you very well.

Would you want that? You must ring her back, please. Then you must join me for a cup of tea and tell me all about the burglary.'

It was characteristic of her, Olivia approved, that she had not rushed into that first.

'A policeman paid me a social visit yesterday. The originator of the Mulholland Bolt, I understand. I was flattered. Besides yourself, Olivia, my path is rarely crossed by the great. Though I have one small objection: that you did not leave me a note informing me of what had occurred. As I believe I stated on another occasion, you must not think it your duty to shield an old woman from the terrors of this world. And should you aspire to do so, a square of cardboard in a door is hardly adequate. However, I forgive you. Meanwhile I think we should apply our minds to more serious kinds of protection. You make that telephone call, then we can discuss them.'

'How was it?' Judy demanded.

'Not bad. I was exhausted when I arrived, but recovered. You know, the usual adrenalin. How's the play going?'

'Picking up. The producer has let it be known that for the time being his suicide is postponed. Are you still affected, then, by the break-in?'

'No, by the day after. It's too long a story for now, Judy, but I'm sure they're both safe.'

'Both?'

'Yes. Not only Rita but Elizabeth. I'm reasonably certain that there were attacks on her similar to those on me. She runs a sort of unofficial refuge, which can have no chance of remaining a secret in this town, so the husbands know about it. I've been in the house and I found a letter. It was opened, from Rita, and explained that she'd gone off with her real father. So Elizabeth must have left after that. It was the wisest course since the heat was on.'

'I hope it's off you.'

'So do I, but if it isn't, at least there'll be no surprises; and I could probably evade it – try a new colour rinse, throw away this sweat-shirt, find a different image. Elizabeth's is too much of a strain.'

'Don't be facetious, Olivia.'

'I'm not being, entirely. Obviously I should be safe if I didn't have such a provocative double.'

'A false nose and whiskers wouldn't be enough to put off those who've already identified you and know where you're living.'

'You mean the telephone freak?' Two days ago she had assured Judy that the kerb crawler had not reappeared. 'I think he's probably given up. I haven't received a call since Wednesday.' Thanks to the exchange.

'Sounds promising; but I was also referring to the burglar.'

'Yes. I don't think that one will break in again. It was very bright of you, Judy, to suspect that wasn't a spontaneous mess; it was made, as far as possible, on the model of the programme. As a punishment – for either me or Elizabeth. Probably the person wasn't sure which. The room on "Mystery of the Week" was hers, you see, not Rita's. Steve always thought there was something strange about that part of the film. It didn't match the room he remembered.'

'But you shouldn't assume that you're out of danger,' Judy persisted. 'I'm not thinking only of the break-in.'

'I may not be, but the harassment seems to be cyclical. There was a reference to it in Rita's letter, something like: "it stopped before for a bit", as if there are calmer patches between crises. Please don't worry. Look, the problem will be solved if the Piccolo offers me the part. Otherwise, I'll sort something out. I have the impression that Mrs Winterton is about to propose measures to suit a state of emergency – what did you say to her? – and I can always call upon Steve or Earl. Except that neither has much credibility as a bodyguard. It's Elizabeth that needs protection, Judy, and I shall keep an eye on her house and visit her when she returns.'

'Will you? I can appreciate the reason, yet what a bizarre meeting!' Reunion, Olivia silently corrected. 'But I suppose you won't be in any greater danger than you have been in this week. Which reminds me of that man in Greasy Len's. I can't understand why he was so outraged at your being with a chap who was black.'

'I don't think it was Earl's colour that was the problem. There had been a newspaper report following the film.' About to describe the few seconds they had missed, she paused. She could not repeat those improvised lines of a man Judy had once loved. She could not let the other know that one cause of her being victimized this past week was their friendship. She said, 'I didn't see the report until Friday. It was nasty. It helped to create an atmosphere, an environment, which encouraged what happened. It was based on delusions and prejudice. Whose target was me.'

'Oh, my dear. Look, why don't you trundle over and tell me at leisure? See the play, too. You can stay as long as you wish.'

'I'd love to, and I'll come very soon; but not now. I've already arranged to visit Mum and Dad. Tomorrow. After I've taken some things out of pawn.' To redeem them would require all the fee for 'Mystery of the Week'. Such a use seemed appropriate.

'Heavens. "That it should come to this!" Whatever could you pawn?'

'Nothing; but someone else managed it. And I intend to return the loot to its owner before I go home.'